TALL, DARK AND DELICIOUS

Consuelo would have continued, but Ramón's strong arms quickly grabbed her and pulled her close. His mouth came down in a punishing kiss that took her by surprise. She struggled to push him away. She could feel the heat of his body as her heart pounded against his chest. Finally, she went limp and his mouth relaxed, becoming more gentle and exploring. He'd always had the power to make her go weak with a mere touch. Now, after so long without him, her senses came alive and she returned his kiss. . . .

TALL, DARK AND DELICIOUS

Reyna Rios

PINNACLE BOOKS
Kensington Publishing Corp.
http://www.encantoromance.com

*In legends it is said that the rainbow
is the bridge between heaven and earth.*

*For my daughter Anamari, "Tweedy,"
who is every color of the rainbow.*

Prologue

1969

"He came to her home and with him was a priest. He confessed that he'd separated from his regiment and would need to return soon after they married.

"With love in her eyes, she followed him outside and to a nearby tree—an oak in its prime. He promised her a church wedding later. 'For now, this will have to do,' he told her with great sadness in his eyes.

"That's where the soldiers found them. They chained him, but before they took him away, one of the soldiers spat at her feet. 'We will clean your memory of this traitor!' he shouted as he set fire to her home and the tree.

"As they led her lover away, he cried out, 'If there's a way, I'll return to you. Wait for me, my love.'

"With time and the help of the townspeople, she rebuilt her home.

"And she waited.

"The wind carried her lonely prayer, through

trees, through mountains and sky. One night, while she knelt where the tree had stood, she thought she heard an owl call her name. Surely it was a sign. After that, whenever she heard the owl, she came to think of him as her guardian and messenger.

"Years passed and her faith remained. Only once did it waver. For weeks the owl did not show up. Instead of praying, she cried out the chant of her ancestors . . . the chant of sorrow.

"Eventually the owl returned and she resumed her prayers.

"Suddenly, at the spot where the tree had burned to the ground, a root took sprout and, to the amazement of everyone, there grew two trees from one root.

"She saw it as the sign she had prayed for. The tree had died and now returned to life. And so would she.

"Shortly after, her lover returned. They were no longer young and they cried and held each other, for it was enough that their love had survived and they'd been reunited.

"He looked deeply into her eyes and said, 'You were in every breath I took, and I drank of every tear you shed.'

"On their wedding day as they stood beneath the tree—for she refused to be married anywhere else—the people of Sandera swore that while the marriage vows were being said, the tree took on a burning aura."

Salvador Medina's voice took on an excited whisper. "And they were married beneath this very tree where we sit."

"Oh, Daddy, tell us another story. Pleeeze?" cried Lara, his youngest.

He warmed to his subject again. "And that's why every June we celebrate our Annual Shrine Festival, so the unmarried ladies of Sandera can march from the church to this spot in order to ask the saints to help guide their soul mates to them."

"What's a soul mate?" asked Gordy, his son.

"It's that one special person who is meant only for you, if you're lucky enough to find each other."

"Who told you the story, Daddy?" asked Lara, ever the curious one.

"My father and his father before him."

"Daddy, will I run to this shrine someday so my sun mate can find me?"

Her father laughed and hugged her. "It's *soul* mate, Larita, not sun. And who knows? Perhaps you will, God willing. For now though, I hear your mother calling. So scat, I'll be in to kiss you good night in a moment."

One

The Texas sun had barely made its presence known, but already Sandera tongues were wagging as excited murmurs made their way from one end of town to the other. No one knew who had started the rumor, only that the mailman had gotten into the act by stopping at every vendor's door to spread the word. As gossip grew more frenzied, the majority of interested citizens rubbed their hands together in anticipation. Things were about to heat up.

Ramón Santos was back in town.

"And just in time for the Annual Shrine Festival," one of the Sanchez twins told Lena Morales as they arrived at the bakery.

"That" should cause many a single woman's heart to beat faster," Lena replied, thinking of her own unmarried daughter. "Don't you think?"

Lidia Sanchez nodded. "As well as a couple of married ones, too."

"Do you think Consuelo knows?" Lidia asked the baker as he was unlocking his door.

He took off his cap and scratched his head. ¿*"Quien sabe?"* He shrugged. "But if she doesn't know now, she will soon," he added, giving her a meaningful look. But Lidia didn't notice because at that moment she stopped a passerby, and the line of communication continued to spread.

Standing near the edge of the Concho River, in the cool tranquility of her snug retreat, where shadows hung from oaks like curtains, Consuelo Rodriquez took a deep breath. The spring dawn smelled of thawed earth, and she watched in fascination as the sun rose, painting the eastern sky a delicate rose color. She shivered slightly when a cool breeze blew off the river and lifted her hair.

Consuelo fought the temptation to stretch out and relax on the soft, green earth, surrounded by wildflowers in all their color frenzy. She wanted to wallow in the peaceful, idyllic scene but resisted and turned her attention to the reason she'd come here.

She walked over to a well-worn spot, the proof she'd been coming here for the past three years. Propped up against an old log was a large, brown grocery bag. She reached inside, took out six empty milk cartons, and stood them on the log. Placed wide apart, they looked like sentries at attention.

Consuelo walked several feet away and turned to study the cartons. She took in a breath, let it out, then grabbed the coiled whip hanging from her belt and snapped it with a swift, smooth swing. The whip uncoiled in an arc and snared one of the cartons. With a quick jerk, she yanked it back, then did the same with the others.

She smiled, recalling her friend Josie's interested gaze when she'd spotted the whip hanging on her bedroom wall. Consuelo had laughingly confessed that ever since she'd seen Michelle Pfeiffer's expert use of the whip in a *Batman* movie, she'd been obsessed with learning how to use it. And she'd gotten damn good at it.

When she finished practicing with the cartons, she dipped into the sack again, brought out six cola cans, and did the same with them. However, the whip barely licked the last can, and it shuddered for a second before toppling over. When it happened again later, Consuelo frowned. Her aim was off today and she knew why.

Ramón had been home for two weeks. Two weeks! And he hadn't come to see her. And why should he? she thought. They hadn't exactly parted on happy terms. Other than a couple short glances during her best friend Josie's wedding almost two years ago, she hadn't seen him for seven years. She'd been protected from any personal contact with him by a throng of people, and then he was gone. He'd probably attended the reception for only about fifteen minutes.

She stared ahead at pasture and trees. Almost everything that had any importance in her life could be traced to this spot. It had been here, where she stood now, that she and Ramón had made plans to marry.

Only she'd married someone else.

Regret hung over her like a dark cloud. Regret

that she hadn't followed her heart, and remorse over the fact that she felt she'd had no other choice at the time.

Ironically, she stood on Santos land. The three brothers—Ramón, the eldest; Rafael; and Raul—owned the ranch land together. She'd always loved this spot. Here, she and Ramón had laughed and loved together. This small corner of the world had been theirs for a time.

Closing her eyes, she felt a sudden stab of longing as an image of their bodies joined together floated across her memory, and then, just as quickly, she pushed the memory aside, locking it away again.

The calming sound of moving water drew her gaze to the river. If she'd wanted to forget him, this had been the wrong place to come.

She sighed and began picking up cartons and cans, pitching them back into the sack. After she placed the sack and whip in the car, she glanced toward the river again. Usually, she took a quick dip after her practice session, and today the crystal-clear water looked especially inviting.

She reached down to unbutton her blouse, then changed her mind. Duty called. She couldn't put off going over the books any longer.

As she climbed into her car, Consuelo wondered if she should find another place to practice. Raul had given her permission to come here anytime she chose, but now that Ramón had returned Consuelo wasn't sure she'd be welcome anymore. She started the engine and, as she headed toward the main road, took one last look around.

Maybe she wouldn't have to stop coming here. Maybe he wouldn't find out.

And maybe crows would turn white.

On a ridge some distance away, a black stallion pawed the ground. His rider, equally as restless, watched Consuelo from beneath an oak shawled in strands of Spanish moss. As he watched her pitch the last can into the sack, he wondered what had possessed him to come here today. Maybe it was because he'd missed seeing the beauty of his land, or perhaps he'd just wanted to visit this particular spot again. Whatever his reason, he certainly hadn't expected to see *her* here.

He had to admit she was still beautiful; her hourglass figure was a little rounder, fuller in places, but it agreed with her. Her body, silhouetted against the rising sun, looked as though she and the dawn were trying to outdo each other.

His eyes swept over her again. Tucked into her snug black jeans was a sleeveless red shirt adorned with rhinestones on the collar and pockets, and encircling her small waist lay a silver hip-slung belt. A flat-crowned, black Western hat sat low on her head, and snuggled halfway inside the hatband was an eagle feather. As the sun climbed higher, it lit her skin and made it glow like soft amber.

Seven years fell away as he conjured up the summer day he'd given her that feather, and what they had done afterward. Beneath the hat, her beautiful midnight hair hung straight, reaching almost to her waist. Scarlet Western boots completed her outfit.

He'd been faintly amused as he'd watched her using the whip, but a moment later felt a grudging respect for her. She was good. Very good.

By now, she was probably wondering why he hadn't been to see her. He'd asked himself that same question. It wasn't that he didn't want to. He did, but he wanted it to be in his own good time and on his own terms.

As Consuelo drove away, the stallion snorted and pawed the ground again.

"I see you're as restless as I am, Diablo. Let's go." He made a mental note of the day—Thursday—as he spurred the stallion homeward.

Pushing open the back door that led to the kitchen, Consuelo continued up the stairs.

She had owned Consuelo's Mexican Restaurant for the past six years. Not wanting to travel the distance back and forth to her mother's home, she had turned the upstairs into an apartment since she sometimes worked late into the night. Owning the restaurant had been her salvation and had kept her busy through the lonely months after her husband Tomas's death.

Twenty minutes later, she took one last peek in the full-length mirror on her closet door to make sure her slip didn't show under the bright red uniform, which consisted of a full skirt and a peasant blouse that could be worn on or off the shoulder. She'd had the same uniform made for her female employees, while the male waiters wore black pants and red shirts.

She had an hour before the restaurant opened at eleven—time enough to plan the day and visit with Tía Juana, who was also her cook. Consuelo hurried down the stairs to the kitchen, taking in the familiar clatter of dishes and enticing aroma of cooking meat and spices.

Juana looked up from her daily ritual of making tortillas and nodded a greeting.

"Hola, Tía. How's it going?"

"Bien. But you look tired. Are you getting any sleep?"

"Yes," she lied, grabbing a flour tortilla and biting into it. "You know I'm a regular night owl. I'll be fine."

Juana looked skeptical. "Maybe you should see a doctor."

"Goodness, Tía, do I look *that* bad? You're going to give me a complex." Wanting to change the subject, Consuelo asked, "How about you? Everything all right here?"

"Fine," Juana replied. "Although if too many more people quit eating out, we're going to be in trouble."

It was true that business had slowed down a bit, but Consuelo was confident it would pick up again.

"Don't worry. We've weathered bad times before."

"If you say so," Juana said as she took a pan out from under the counter, filled it with water, and began pouring pinto beans into it.

For a moment, Consuelo was filled with a sense of uneasiness. Maybe she shouldn't confide in her aunt too much. But then Juana was the only person Consuelo trusted. She'd been a second mother to her, more so since she'd helped Consuelo through a couple of the worst years of her life.

Two of her waiters, Enrique and Sophia, entered the kitchen, saving Consuelo the trouble of having to reply to her aunt.

"Sophia, I'll act as hostess until you relieve me around two, okay?"

"Sure," Sophia said as she put her purse away. Consuelo always opened the restaurant at eleven, worked until three or so, then took off for a few hours and returned at six until the restaurant closed at ten. Sometimes she worked on through, as she would today to go over the books.

As the day wore on, the traffic of people filtered in and out until slowly the sun began to fade. At eight o'clock, Enrique walked past Consuelo as she sat in the kitchen eating her dinner. Carrying a tray, he stopped and said, "I'm delivering this to Señora Morales and her daughter, so if I'm not back in a few minutes, come get me."

Consuelo grinned. Lena Morales had a habit of chatting too much, which tended to make people nervous . . . especially Enrique, who usually got caught waiting on her table. Her daughter Esperanza was just the opposite—quiet and shy. It was amazing how two people could be so close and yet so different.

Consuelo continued eating, but every now and then she glanced at Juana. Finally, she asked, "Tía, do you ever get tired of cooking all the time? I mean, are you happy?" She didn't know why she'd asked. Maybe because she felt so restless these days.

Her aunt looked surprised. "Me? *Sí, cómo no.* Why do you ask?"

Consuelo rose and took her empty plate over to the sink. "Just wondering. You work pretty hard around here. And I was thinking." She turned to face Juana. "If you need extra time off for any reason, I'll understand."

Juana's dark eyes narrowed suspiciously over her plump olive cheeks. "And why would I want to do that?"

Consuelo shrugged. "I just want you to know that I appreciate all you do around here and if you need some time off for any reason, you can take it. Paid vacation, of course," she politely tacked on.

Juana picked up a large wooden spoon and stirred the beans. "If I decide to take off, I'll let you know. You'd better go rescue Enrique."

Consuelo peeked through the small glass window of the kitchen door and spied Lena Morales chattering nonstop, her hands moving in quick birdlike gestures. As Consuelo headed for their table, she wondered how long Lena could talk without stopping to catch her breath.

Enrique looked relieved when he saw her. Esperanza glanced up and smiled sweetly.

"Oh, hello, Consuelo," Lena said. "I was just telling Enrique he should go to TSU."

Consuelo smiled. "I'm sure Enrique will make the right decision when the time comes. And how are you two ladies this evening?" she said, steering the conversation away from Enrique. He threw her a grateful look and hurried back to the kitchen.

"Never better. We've been shopping today."

"Sounds exciting. I'd better let you two eat before your food gets cold."

"Wait!" Lena shouted.

Consuelo turned.

"I suppose you know Ramón is back, *verdad?*"

Consuelo nodded as she met Lena's speculative glance.

"Didn't you two date in high school?"

"Yes, for a while." The dating had continued long after high school, but she wasn't about to fuel Lena's imagination.

"Oh, my dear, he's such a nice man."

And a bachelor, Consuelo thought, smiling at Esperanza. "Yes, he always was. Excuse me, I have to make a call."

"Oh, but I have some news," Lena said. When Consuelo made no move to leave, Lena continued excitedly, "We . . . Esperanza, that is, invited him to our home for dinner next Thursday and he accepted. Has he eaten here? Do you know what his favorite food is?"

Consuelo considered the question. "I wish I

could be more help, but it's been a long time since I've seen Ramón. I'm sure his tastes have changed since then."

Lena aimed a wide smile at Consuelo. "Well, no matter. We may ask one of his brothers. Or better yet, we'll visit Ramón across the street. You know he bought Salvador's building, don't you?" She glanced around to see if anyone else was listening, then lowered her voice an octave. "Of course, it's probably just a tax write-off. I have it on good authority that he's been buying up property around here with plans to develop it."

Consuelo shifted uneasily. "That's interesting, Lena, but you know, even if he does build on the land, he doesn't necessarily have to remain here. He can pick up and move on to the next project any time he chooses. He can work from anywhere."

"Yes, but he told us he's setting up his office in that building, and just think, it's right across the street from you. I'm surprised he hasn't told you," Lena ended on a curious note.

Consuelo shrugged. "He's probably been busy. Well, ladies, I wish you luck with the dinner." Consuelo's smile didn't quite reach her eyes. A stab of something closely resembling jealousy surprised her. She was pretty certain Lena was trying to find Esperanza a husband, and the fact that Ramón was a bachelor *and* rich was no doubt enough to make Lena drool.

Lena winked conspiratorially. "She'd be lucky to snag such a catch as Ramón, don't you think?"

"Mother, please, you're embarrassing me," Esperanza said, smiling shyly at Consuelo.

Relieved to be spared from replying, Consuelo returned the smile. "I'd better get you more tea. Be right back, ladies."

After quickly refilling their tea glasses, Consuelo stopped Enrique on his way to another table. "Tell Juana that if she needs me, I'll be in my office."

Consuelo was about to enter her office when the hostess approached.

"Raul just called and made reservations for a homecoming dinner party for Ramón Saturday night."

"For how many?"

"Ten."

Something flickered in Consuelo's eyes. "Put them in the toucan room."

A minute later, Consuelo closed the door behind her, then went over and sat down at her desk. She picked up a letter opener and proceeded to open the stack of mail on her desk. Soon there were three stacks of opened mail in front of her: junk mail, receipts, and invoices. She opened her top drawer, reached in, and took out her checkbook, then began to write out a check for each invoice.

Fifteen minutes later, she glared at the check in her hand in frustration. Twice she'd made a mistake in the dollar amount. Leaning back, she closed her eyes. Saturday was only two days away. Sandera was a small town; she knew that eventually she and Ramón would run into each other, especially if he was going to be across the street every day. But now the thought of actually seeing him in two days, made her uneasy.

Would he speak to her? she wondered.

Finding it difficult to concentrate, she looked out the window just in time to see Esperanza and her mother leave the restaurant. Esperanza was a pretty girl in her early twenties, perhaps a little young for Ramón, who was thirty-six. But then what did age matter in affairs of the heart?

A vision of Ramón having dinner with Esperanza made Consuelo frown. She could well imagine the welcome Ramón would get from Lena. He would enter her elegant dining room, where the table would be set with delicate white china, crystal glasses, and shiny silverware. Once they were seated, Lena would most likely make some excuse that she'd forgotten to return an important phone call and leave her daughter in charge. Across the candlelit table, Esperanza would turn her innocent eyes toward Ramón.

Consuelo blinked and grabbed another invoice.

He certainly hadn't wasted any time, she thought, somewhat miffed.

She gazed at the invoice in her hand and stared at it for so long her eyes grew tired. Finally, her eyelashes fluttered closed and she drifted off.

TWO

His sunbaked body lay before her, strong and powerful-looking, with thickly muscled shoulders—testimony of a man who was used to working outdoors.

An evocative smile turned up the corners of her mouth and her eyes danced at the erotic sight before her. She wanted to say something, but his raw, masculine beauty held her spellbound. In the background, the strains of a Spanish ballad filled the air and a woman's husky voice joined in, her words full of the passion and longing of unrequited love. But it was the singer's suffering tone that shook her more than the words.

She swayed with the music as she stood behind the counter in her kitchen. She wore nothing but an apron boldly patterned with a leopard print, its ruffled lacing barely covering her breasts. Her nipples strained against the soft, cotton fabric as she felt them swell. Inhaling, she caught the scent of his woodsy aftershave as it mingled with the more pungent aromas of cumin, freshly cut rosemary, and oregano. She glanced at him again as he lay on the counter, looking faintly amused but silent.

She blinked. Suddenly he had shrunk until his body was barely the length of a spoon. And he was lying on a tortilla.

As the last sad strains of music melted into silence, the wall clock softly chimed midnight. Tossing her hair over her shoulder, she scooped up the bottle of salsa and spooned some over his body, then slathered guacamole on top and rolled him up in the tortilla. She opened her mouth and—

"Consuelo!"

Consuelo frowned. A thumping somewhere near her head kept getting louder.

"Consuelo! *Despierta, hija.* Wake up," the voice repeated.

Slumped over, with her elbow propped on the desk and her palm cradling her head, Consuelo jumped slightly, slowly opened one eye, and saw Juana's face peering down at her.

"*Caramba,* that's the second time this week you've fallen asleep in here. Why don't you go on up to bed?"

Consuelo straightened and yawned. "I'm fine, just a little tired. Did you need something?"

Juana peered at her more closely. "It's closing time."

Startled, Consuelo glanced at the wall clock. Ten P.M. "I must've lost track of time."

"Are you certain you're all right?"

"I'm positive. I'll be up front in a minute."

"I'll be glad to close up, if you want."

"*Gracias,* Tía, but that won't be necessary. I'm wide awake now. Why don't you go on home?"

"If you're sure you don't need me." Juana still didn't sound convinced as she leaned down to pick up an invoice that had fluttered to the floor.

"No. Please go. I'll see you tomorrow."

After Juana had closed the door behind her, Consuelo blinked the sleep out of her eyes and sighed. She'd dreamed of Ramón again. The second time this week. The first dream had been just as ridiculous as this one. Good God, they'd been frolicking in a vat of warm chocolate.

Consuelo put her checkbook away, locked the top drawer, and rose. She had to quit thinking about him. And she had to stop expecting him to walk through her door just to come see her.

That must be it, she thought with sudden insight. Tonight her dream must have been a message that she was upset with Ramón. After all, one didn't forget the love of their life, did they? *She* certainly hadn't.

When she entered the main dining room, Enrique was vacuuming.

"Why don't you go on home, Enrique? There haven't been enough people here today to mess up the floor."

"Must be spring fever. People are thinking of other things besides food," he teased.

Consuelo smiled. "How's school?"

He shrugged. "Fine. I have finals coming up next week."

"In that case, you'd better go home and get some sleep. Come on, I'll walk you out."

Putting the vacuum cleaner away, he said, "You don't have to do that."

"I have to lock up anyway, so I'll just say good-bye at the door."

He grabbed his schoolbooks and followed her

to the door. There, she held it open until he got into his car and started the engine.

She was just about to close up when a sound made her jump. It was faint at first, then louder. She'd heard that sound before. It was the unmistakable mewling of a kitten. Consuelo peeked around the door to get a better look. The full moon outlined a black kitten. He crouched just to the right of the door. If Consuelo had swung the door wider, she would've hit him.

Forgetting Enrique, she walked over and looked down at the feline. It couldn't have been more than six weeks old.

"Don't tell me. You got dumped, right?"

He rubbed against her ankle.

"Don't you try to ankle-polish your way into my good graces, because it's not going to work." She felt his rough tongue licking her skin and she flinched. "Ooh, stop that."

As she bent over and picked him up, his motorized purr grew louder and he settled himself more comfortably against her chest.

"Well, maybe for one meal . . . but that's all."

She held him up so she could look into his eyes. "And we'd better get something straight right now. There's absolutely no place in my heart for a little vagabond like you, you got that?"

The feline meowed and closed his eyes, then purred louder as she hugged him to her chest.

"I don't think he believes you," a male voice said from behind her.

Startled, Consuelo whirled around, almost dropping the kitten.

"Ramón!" His name tore from her throat in surprise. *Dios mío, I'm not ready for this,* she thought. "You frightened me half to death," she said and glanced around nervously.

"You should be more careful out here. I might have been a thief or worse."

He *was* much worse, she thought as a slight tremor started somewhere in the pit of her stomach. A thief might've made her heart pound with fear, but he wouldn't have made it hurt like it was doing now.

The kitten balked at being held too tightly and struggled in her grip. She stared at Ramón, not knowing what else to say.

His cool green eyes were fixed on the cat before they lifted to meet hers. "I think he's getting a little impatient. Why don't you invite me in so you can feed him?"

She wondered if he was really talking about the cat or himself.

"Sure. Come on in," she said. "I was just about to close." She'd waited for this day, had imagined that someday, out of the blue, she would turn and he'd be there, and of course, his eyes would smile, letting her know he'd missed her. But he wasn't smiling and she was at a loss as to what to say.

"You sure it's all right? I don't want to keep you from anything."

"Yes, I'm certain," she said. "Come on."

She led him to the kitchen, where she took a saucer from a cupboard and set it on the counter.

"Would you like something to drink?" With the kitten in one arm, she took the milk carton out of the fridge with the other and poured some into the saucer.

"I'll pass on the drink, but I'd like a tour of your place."

"All right," she said, setting the kitten and the saucer on the floor. The feline sniffed the milk, then began to lap it up.

"That should keep him quiet for a while. You didn't by any chance plant this cat on my doorstep, did you?" Her hands trembled slightly as she returned the milk to the fridge.

His sensual mouth lifted in a smile and he shook his head. "No way." The slashes on each side of his mouth deepened, causing her to remember how that mouth had once been full of passion and laughter. She looked away.

"You've seen the kitchen, so let's go in the main dining room."

Except for the kitchen light, most of the overhead lights had been turned off, leaving only the soft glow of accent lighting from walls and several candles that hadn't been snuffed out yet.

His interest was evident as he glanced around the room, from the *saltillo*-tiled floor to the grouping of photographs mounted on the wall. He walked over and studied one of the photos. It was a group picture of Consuelo, Ramón, and his two brothers, Rafael and Raul. They were all laughing as they posed for the camera.

And as he studied the pictures, she studied him, letting her gaze travel over the hard planes of his body, admiring the way his muscles rippled across his shoulders and forearms. He exuded the masculine strength and natural beauty of a man who was used to doing physical work.

His hands were large, the fingers long. He was tall, six-foot-one. His chocolate-colored hair was longer than she'd remembered it, falling way past his neck, almost to his shoulders. She'd once told him how much she loved Mel Gibson's long, wavy hair and he'd teased her, telling her *she* should wear it that way. But in the next instant, when she'd agreed, he had run his hands through her hair, and before pulling her mouth to his for a kiss, he'd made her promise she would never cut it.

He finally looked up. "That was a lifetime ago."

There was nothing she could do but nod her head in agreement.

He shifted his attention to the double glass doors that led to an inner courtyard, where a garden fountain stood as sentinel, surrounded by potted flowers and plants.

"There's a separate room in the back for smokers, although most of them eat outside on the patio if the weather permits. That hall to the left leads to two rooms, one for a large party and a smaller room for private dinner parties. It isn't huge by Texas standards but it's intimate and comfortable. Would you like to look at it?"

"I'll see it another time."

Consuelo shifted uncomfortably. Having him stand so close to her brought back memories that filled her with longing. He had always stirred her in a way no other man ever had nor would ever be able to.

Her face flushed and she looked away. What would he say if he knew she'd dreamed of him in the buff earlier? Something stirred within her. He stood so close she could make out a small scar on his chin and wondered how it had gotten there.

His brothers both had hazel eyes, more amber, but Rafael had inherited green eyes from his mother. They weren't emerald, but more the color of a dark, stormy sea.

She was so engrossed in watching him that she jumped nervously when he turned that intense gaze on her. He regarded her quizzically, then nodded approvingly. "I like your place."

"Thanks." She wanted to tell him how much it meant to her to hear him say that, but she held back.

"It's getting late. You probably want to go home."

She smiled. "I *am* home. I live upstairs."

He seemed genuinely surprised. "Seems like you thought of everything, but then you always were an enterprising lady."

She wondered if he'd meant it as a compliment or if he was mocking her. "It beats having to drive back and forth to work every day. It's adequate and it suits me just fine."

He nodded. "You've done all right."

"From what I've heard, so have you." At his curious glance, she added, "You must've liked Chicago; you were gone a long time."

He shrugged. "My business partner lived there. After we were discharged from the service, I agreed to move to his home base. A bigger city suited me more at the time."

"I heard you bought Salvador's building and properties."

He grinned, shaking his head ruefully. "I'd forgotten how fast news travels in a small town. You probably know more about my business than I do."

Her eyes danced. She was tempted to tell him that she even knew about his dinner date with Esperanza. "If you'll remember, there isn't much else to do around here. Our identities are closely tied to family, church, and the ordinary events of daily life such as birth, courtship, marriage, old age . . . and death," she added sadly.

"That's a mouthful. Makes me want to make sure I use my time wisely." When she didn't respond, he shifted his attention away from her to glance around the room again. "In any case, it seems congratulations are in order."

"*Gracias*, I've survived."

He looked at her oddly. "That's an interesting way of putting it."

She shifted uneasily again. "I simply meant that life isn't always so simple. Sometimes we have to muddle through."

"And did you?"

"Did I what?"

"Muddle through."

"I managed. Would you like something from the bar?"

"Why, Connie, do I detect life in those dark eyes of yours?"

He was goading her. "Not at all, Ramón. I was only thinking that you didn't stay in town long enough to know what I was feeling." There, she'd said it. It was out in the open.

His own eyes narrowed. "I left because there was no longer any reason for me to stay."

She felt her chest tighten. Now that she'd brought out a part of their past, she regretted it. It was, after all, their first visit in years.

She decided it would be safer to change the subject. "I'm sorry your father passed away."

"Yeah. I heard your father died also." There was no remorse, no pity in his voice; he was merely stating a fact. He might as well have been asking about the weather.

"Yes. There was nothing anyone could do. By that time the cancer had spread too far."

"At least he lived long enough to see you married and settled." His voice sounded hollow.

She crossed her arms defensively. "I attended your father's funeral, but I guess you didn't see me."

"I left town right after."

"I figured as much."

"Does it surprise you I'm back?"

"A little."

"No one knows better than you, Connie, how important family is. I miss my brothers, and I've earned the right to work from any location I want."

She swallowed painfully. "Yes, I would do anything for my family."

His face remained blank, but something in his eyes flickered. "As I recall, you did. You gave up your freedom."

The silence stretched awkwardly between them.

He leaned lazily against the door frame, his arms folded across his chest. "I've often wondered. Was it worth it?"

For a moment, her eyes brimmed over and she fought to hold on to her tears and her dignity.

"At the time, I did what I thought was best."

"And now?"

"It doesn't really matter what I think now. I can't change the past." Her face and voice were bland.

As if tiring of the conversation, he straightened and shrugged. "You're right. Actually, I also came here for another reason." At her guarded look, he said, "My brothers and a few friends are throwing me a dinner party Saturday night."

"Yes, I know. Raul called."

"They've always liked you, and I don't want them feeling uncomfortable on my part. I came here to negotiate a peace treaty."

"I wasn't aware we were at war."

"A bad choice of words on my part. I'm simply asking that we put the past behind us. I don't want either of us to feel uncomfortable every time we run into each other. My brothers would pick up on it immediately."

Consuelo looked away. She was afraid that if she looked into his eyes, she might be tempted to tell him just how close she'd come to leaving her family, to committing the ultimate sin by running off with him.

But she said none of those things. It would do her no good now.

"How long do you plan to stay in town?" she asked.

"As far as I know, indefinitely."

But if Consuelo was nothing else, she was a consummate actress. "In that case, you have no need to fear that I'll embarrass you or make you feel uncomfortable in any way." She smiled. "And I agree to your peace treaty. I'll even shake on it if you like."

She offered him her palm, and he took it in his larger one. His hand felt rough, warm, and familiar.

"To peace?" she asked.

"Peace," he replied, smiling. "And I hope you'll accept my invitation to join us."

For a moment, she was thrown off guard. She hadn't expected him to invite her. "I . . . thank you for the invitation."

"Come lock the door. I have to go."

As she walked him to the door, she realized that he'd never mentioned anything about being friends.

She watched Ramón leave with a mixture of excitement and depression. By the time she reached the kitchen, depression had won out.

She picked up the kitten and cooed to him. Now that his tummy was full, his sleepy eyes told her in no uncertain terms that he hadn't appreciated her waking him.

"I'm sorry, sweetie, but I need you where I can keep an eye on you. I don't want you to get trampled when people start arriving tomorrow."

She carried him upstairs and set him down next

to her bed, then laid some newspaper close to the bathroom. It was the best she could do for now. She went to her kitchen and brought back a small bowl filled with water and set it down beside him.

She felt a lingering despondency as she slipped on her gown. By the time she sat before the oval mirror to brush her hair, a deep ache settled in her chest. She couldn't bear the thought of seeing him again. It would hurt too much.

She had dreamed of this day for years, had pictured Ramón's homecoming a thousand times in her mind, had imagined every little detail down to the part where he would reach out and draw her into his embrace. In his eyes she would see how much he still cared for her, and then he would kiss her. She always replayed that scene, over and over, like the rewinding of a videotape.

But life has no rewind button, she thought sadly as she laid the brush down. She'd allowed herself the fantasies because they were what had kept her going.

She stared at her reflection again and wondered if he'd noticed the dark smudges under her eyes. She hadn't been sleeping well, and it was beginning to show.

She glanced down at the kitten, who sat looking so tiny, so vulnerable, watching her.

"Yeah, I know I look awful," she said as she slipped into bed.

In that brief moment just before she turned out the light, she knew without a doubt that she wanted Ramón back.

The instant the light went out and she closed

her eyes, the kitten uttered an indignant cry and his tiny, sharp claws latched on to the bedspread. He hoisted himself up the side of the bed and crawled over to lie on her chest.

Consuelo yawned, stroking the cat's fur, and whispered in the dark. "Don't get too comfortable. Tomorrow I'm finding you a home." At his answering purr, she said, "But I promise you'll be happy with my choice."

As she fell into an uneasy sleep, two thoughts kept running through her mind. What did one say to someone she had never stopped loving? And what would it take for her to redeem herself in his eyes?

Across the street, Ramón leaned against the hood of his car and watched the light go out in Consuelo's bedroom. If she had stepped out onto her balcony, she would've seen him.

She'd certainly done well without him, he thought as he studied the two-story adobe structure. The heavy carved door was painted red, which he knew was her favorite color, although the window ledges had been stained a bright turquoise.

Until he'd seen her tonight, he'd almost forgotten the cute way she had of holding her head slightly to one side when she was teasing and the feistiness that shone in her eyes. Her scent was still with him, and he forced himself to look away from her balcony.

He climbed into his car and started the engine.

Somehow, he'd figured he would be satisfied with the way their meeting had gone tonight, but it had left him drained and sad instead. He'd been tempted to dredge up the anger he'd carried around with him for so long, the same anger that had driven him to join the service just after she'd gotten married.

When he'd left town, Ramón had vowed to put any future he might have wanted with her behind him. And he'd succeeded for a while. He never asked about her in his letters or his phone calls home, but it hadn't helped that she'd remained a friend to both his brothers. Rafael and Raul had casually managed to slip her name into their conversations from time to time.

He'd learned to harden his heart against her. His sole reason for coming here tonight had been to let her know that running into each other would be unavoidable. After all, he would be just across the street from her every day, and he didn't want to worry that either of them would feel awkward—for his family's sake.

He had fulfilled his purpose to a point. But he hadn't exactly gotten what he'd come back to town for.

Closure.

For him, there could be nothing else. After all, she'd once made it obvious she had no more use for him. He wouldn't put himself through that hell a second time.

Three

Consuelo could hardly breathe; it felt as if the weight of the world sat smack-dab in the middle of her chest. She opened her eyes slowly and saw two beady eyes watching her intently.

Forgetting she had a houseguest, Consuelo bolted upright, gasping for breath, causing the kitten to roll off her chest and off the bed. Quickly pushing the bedcovers aside, she sat on the edge of the bed and leaned over to pick him up.

"Oh, honey, I'm so sorry. I forgot," she crooned, cradling him in her arms and stroking his fur. Poor little thing; he was so tiny, so fragile. He was lucky he hadn't met with some mishap in the parking lot. For an instant, she seethed with anger at the blatant streak of cruelty of whoever had dumped him on her doorstep.

Assuring herself he was all right, she offered him her sweetest smile. The kitten blinked his eyes as though she'd hurt his feelings. She nuzzled him with her chin, then set him on her lap, reached for the phone, and punched in her sister's number.

When she had her on the phone, she simply

said, "Luna, I need to talk to you as soon as possible. Can you come by this morning?" Before her sister could protest, Consuelo said, "It's important."

An hour later, Luna stood in the middle of Consuelo's bedroom, muttering, "What's the rush?"

"I'm going to need you for the next couple of days, especially tomorrow night. I took reservations for a dinner party."

Luna, spotting the kitten lying next to the bed, went over and picked it up. "For a moment, I thought you were going to agree to double-date with me and Mario on Monday night." She kissed the kitten on the nose.

Consuelo stood by the French doors, staring across the street. "I'm too busy to think of dating. Besides, I don't date babies."

Luna stared at her sister as though she'd sprouted horns. "Mario's cousin Hector is my age. Well, perhaps a year younger, twenty-four or twenty-three, I forget."

"That's two years younger than you and, in case you've forgotten, I'm thirty-one."

"Yes, dear sister, but you need to get a life."

Consuelo walked over to the bed and sat down. "I have a life. It's called a business, and it paid for your college tuition."

Luna joined her sister on the bed. "I'm simply saying that you're withering away here. You'd better find a man soon before it's too late."

Consuelo didn't dare ask what it would be too late for. "I don't need a man."

Ignoring her sister, Luna smiled. "Speaking of men, I hear Ramón is back." She watched Consuelo closely.

Consuelo frowned. "Yes, I know. *Everyone* in Sandera knows. And about the dinner party, it's a homecoming dinner for Ramón."

Luna's eyes danced mischievously. "Well now, why didn't you say that to begin with?" She set the kitten on the bed between them.

"I wasn't aware that Ramón was the deciding factor on whether you worked or not."

"He's not. I *am* getting paid, aren't I?"

"Spoken like a true opportunist."

"I learned from the best, Obi-Wan."

"I didn't teach you to be rude."

"No," Luna said quietly. "You just paid my tuition and ignored me for four years."

Consuelo was hurt by the implication. "I was in mourning."

"For four years? Jeez, Connie, it's not like you and Tomas were soul mates or anything."

"What makes you say that?"

Luna hesitated, as though trying to make up her mind about something.

"Spit it out, Luna."

"Because you cried yourself to sleep the night before you married Tomas and I heard you say Ramón's name." At Consuelo's shocked look, Luna added, "I had just gotten home from Vickie's. I didn't want to disturb you, so I went to the living room and waited until you fell asleep."

Consuelo's shoulders tensed. "So that's why you

looked so surprised the next morning when Mother told you I was engaged."

Luna nodded. "*Sí.* I heard you talking to Mami about Ramón later that night, when she assured you you'd made the right choice. I was confused as to why you would marry one man when you loved another, except that I suspected it had something to do with Father."

"Why haven't you said anything before now? Why didn't you ask?"

"I was eighteen years old. I'm asking now. Why did you choose Tomas?"

Consuelo stared at the floor. "It's complicated."

"I think that's my cue to leave." Luna started to rise, but Consuelo reached out and stopped her.

"Father was dying and he was worried about us, especially Mami. His dying wish was that I accept Tomas's proposal so that we would all be taken care of."

"Did Ramón know?"

Consuelo's heart constricted. "I was supposed to meet him at the river that night but Father took a turn for the worse." She absently stroked the kitten's back. "I didn't show up."

Luna looked incredulous. "You mean you didn't tell him why you were marrying Tomas?"

"You knew how ill Father was," Consuelo said in her own defense. "I had to stay with him. Several days later, I called Ramón. By that time he'd heard the news from one of Mother's friends." She folded her hands in her lap. "He refused to speak to me. Later, I heard he'd left town."

Luna gently touched Consuelo's shoulder. "I

know you don't want to hear this, but I wouldn't have married Tomas, no matter what Father said." At Consuelo's cloudy expression, she hastened to add, "I appreciate what you did for me and Mami, but to sacrifice your own happiness? Don't you ever wonder what might've happened if you had chosen Ramón?"

"I didn't have time to think about it," Consuelo lied. "Father died and I was left to take care of the family. Tomas was a good husband, so don't go feeling sorry for me."

Luna sighed deeply. "The only reason I'm saying something now is because . . ."

Consuelo summoned up a smile. "Don't stop now, *hermana*. You've been very vocal up till now."

Luna made a show of studying a bright pink fingernail. "You know how I always pretend to be busy when I'm eavesdropping? People can't tell I'm—"

"Being nosy?"

"Curious," Luna corrected. "It's necessary in order to be a writer."

Consuelo was afraid to ask Luna what she planned to write. "What did you hear?"

Luna turned slightly and leaned back against the headboard. "In the grocery store last night— the wine section—Lena bragged to Berta Leal that Ramón was having dinner with Esperanza next Thursday night and she needed a good red wine. They didn't know I was just around the corner."

"So, what's wrong with that?"

"It was what Berta replied. And I quote, 'Oh,

my dear, he and Consuelo were a hot item at one time. One night on my way to church, I saw them kissing at the town shrine and I thought he was going to swallow her tongue.' "

Consuelo felt her face flush. It was one thing for her and Ramón to have kissed in public, but it was quite another for her little sister to hear about it. . . . "You know good and well that Lena and Berta have always been in competition with each other."

"There's more."

Consuelo rolled her eyes. "I can hardly wait."

Luna grinned. "Lena's eyes took on a thunderous glare as she told Berta that you and Ramón were history; puppy love is what she called it."

The years fell away and Consuelo fought a sudden stab of nostalgia. If she gave into it now, she would be lost. "Lena is right. We *were* young."

Luna shrugged. "That's immaterial now. You should've been there, Sis. Berta's grin would've rivaled a Cheshire cat's. And get a load of this—her answer was: 'That may be, but I wager it's only a matter of time before Consuelo wins him back. After all, the way to a man's heart is through his stomach, and everyone knows Consuelo serves the best food in town. Mark my words, she'll have him eating out of the palm of her hand in no time.' "

Consuelo laughed at Luna's nasal imitation of Berta's voice. "Berta said that?"

"Cross my heart," Luna replied, making a grand gesture of crossing her heart with her index finger.

Consuelo hoped Berta would keep the information to herself. She sighed. The way things were going, it might be too much to hope for.

"Tell you what," Luna said. "I'll spend the night and clean up after the party. It'll give you a break."

Consuelo smiled. "I'd like that. As a matter of fact, I was invited, also."

Luna studied her closely. "You did accept, didn't you?"

"I haven't made up my mind. If I go, I risk an awkward situation."

"If you *don't* go, everyone, including Ramón, will think you're chicken."

Consuelo stood up and set the kitten on the floor. "You have a point. I'll make an appearance."

"Great! Now you're cooking . . . uh, excuse the pun."

"Okay, but don't forget that today is Friday and the dining room will be crowded. Can you stay and work tonight, also?"

"That depends. Can I go home first and grab some clothes and come right back?"

"Of course. Would you like to adopt a cat?"

Luna shook her head. "No way. You're the one who's good with strays, not me. I'd be a terrible mother."

"If I give you some money, would you bring back a litter box?"

"No problem."

Luna reached over and hugged her sister. "Thanks for confiding in me."

Consuelo smiled. "I'm glad we had this chat." And she meant it. Consuelo felt as though a great load had been taken off her shoulders.

Luna, on the other hand, was busy hatching a plot to bring two old lovers together.

Saturday afternoon thunder rumbled against the sky, and Consuelo almost prayed for a storm strong enough to cancel Ramón's dinner party that night, yet in the next instant berated herself for being so selfish. She had no right to wish such things, for she was certain Ramón would have his party with or without her, whether at her restaurant or elsewhere.

Another bolt of lightning danced across the sky, and it began to rain. Consuelo glanced at the wall clock near the entrance as she ushered a couple to a table.

A few minutes later, Enrique approached and handed her a flyer. "I got these from Ramón's office today. He's asking for volunteers to help repair Lupe Espinoza's home next weekend. It's similar to what some of the bigger cities are doing. Twice a year, volunteers go to a run-down section of town and repair homes, most belonging to senior citizens."

Consuelo glanced at the flyer in her hand. "That's very noble of him," she said softly.

Sophia approached. "Luna wants to see you in the kitchen."

Consuelo nodded and turned back to Enrique. "Can I take this and read it later?"

"Sure. Keep it. I have more."

Consuelo headed for the kitchen.

As the afternoon slowly faded, so did the rain. Consuelo wanted to believe that the peaceful blue sky was a sign that everything would go well that night and that she wouldn't make a fool of herself by being too quiet or talking too much. On occasion, when she became overly nervous, she could rival even Lena in the chatterbox department. She closed her eyes and took a deep breath. *Oh God,* she prayed, *please don't let me embarrass myself in any way tonight.*

Someone cleared his throat and Consuelo looked up in time to see a man's impatient stare directed at her. She smiled politely and led him to a table.

When Consuelo stepped through the open French doors of the private dining room at six forty-five, she was already fifteen minutes late. Luna walked beside her.

"How do I look?" she asked Luna.

"Great, although I'd get rid of the jacket. And how in the world do you manage to walk in those shoes? They've got to be at least four inches."

"Three inches and I happen to love them, and not everyone is five-foot-nine like you."

Consuelo noted that everyone stood around the room chatting comfortably. A softly lit chandelier hung in the middle of the room and there were several votive candles placed down the center of a long table that seated twelve people.

Raul was the first to spot them.

"Hi, Consuelo." He leaned over and gave her a strong hug. When he straightened, he turned to Luna but made no move toward her. "Hello, brat." He looked her up and down. "What? No oversize camp shirt or baggy jeans?"

Luna frowned. "Be careful who you call brat, cowboy. When I'm famous, I may just get even."

Consuelo glanced from one to the other. A year ago, for some unexplainable reason, her sister and Raul had taken a dislike to each other.

"Actually, Raul, Luna is working here tonight."

Raul smiled, although the smile didn't quite reach his eyes. "A working college girl. Imagine that!"

Seeing Luna's cloudy expression, Consuelo decided to put a stop to it before her sister really got angry. "Enough, you scoundrel. I want to see Josie. Is she here?"

"I'll see you later," Luna said as she turned on her heel without waiting for a reply.

Consuelo vowed to find out what was going on with those two, but right now her gut was fighting a slow-burning panic.

"*Sí*. Josie's here," Raul said. "And she's been asking about you."

A moment later, Consuelo and Josie exchanged hugs. Consuelo was still grinning as she hugged Josie's husband, Rafael, and their eight-year-old son, Miguel.

"Where's my goddaughter? I want to see her."

Josie's eyes twinkled. "She's right behind you."

Consuelo turned to face the couple who had

just approached. Elena and Diego Castillo were Rafael's ex-in-laws, and even though he and their daughter had been divorced for several years, Rafael considered them family.

Consuelo took Rafaela from Elena and held her, enjoying the feel of her cuddly body and her cooing noises. She was a beautiful baby.

Ben Solis, Ramón's cousin, spoke up. "Hey, you look hot. Wanna come out and see my ranch?"

Consuelo laughed. It was true that Ben had a small spread of land, but nowhere near the size of the Santos brothers'. He'd used that same line on Josie. Of course, she'd had eyes only for Rafael. He'd been her hero in the true sense of the word. When Josie had been mugged and left stranded in Sandera with no transportation or money, Sheriff Rafael Santos had rescued her and her son, and in the process had taken possession of her heart.

"It's good to see you, Ben," Consuelo said.

The baby began to cry. Consuelo kissed her on the cheek and handed her to Josie just as Enrique entered the room with a tray of drinks. He handed one to Consuelo.

"A margarita?" Consuelo wasn't used to drinking except for maybe a little wine on occasion.

"Luna sent it," he replied with a twinkle in his eye.

"Please thank her for me," Consuelo said meaningfully as she raised her glass to toast him.

After a while she began to feel warm, so she set her glass on the table and slipped off her black linen jacket.

Ben gave a low whistle. "Damn, Connie, you look like you were poured into that dress."

Consuelo had chosen to wear an emerald one-shoulder, long-sleeved dress with a wide stretch belt. "Does that mean you like it?" she teased.

"Yep. Sure do."

Shrill laughter drew her attention to the opposite side of the room, and her smile froze in place. Ramón was leaning against the wall listening to Lena Morales. Of course, Esperanza was with her. He had invited them both to his homecoming dinner, which could only mean he was interested in Esperanza.

Disappointment warred with confusion. How could she leave now without being conspicuous? She knew he'd invited her here to keep peace in his family. He'd made that perfectly clear. She also sadly understood that he owed her nothing beyond his generous invitation to join them this evening.

He glanced up and their eyes met and held, and for the space of a heartbeat, Consuelo was caught in the beauty of those green depths. Then Lena stepped in front of him, obscuring him from Consuelo's sight.

She knew now that coming here had been a mistake. How in the world would she get through the evening? With her peripheral vision, she saw him pull away from the wall and head toward her.

"I see you made it." His voice was a low, smooth drawl.

"I don't live far, so it was easy," she teased, attempting to sound natural.

His mouth softened into a lazy smile. "Everyone has already welcomed you, now it's my turn."

She waited for his embrace but it never came. Instead, two strong hands imprisoned her shoulders as he bent down to kiss her on the cheek. Consuelo realized he intended to give her a peck on the cheek and she visibly relaxed. However, in the next instant, his lips moved brazenly forward, coming to rest on the corner of her mouth. Although the action surprised her, it also made her hauntingly aware of another, happier time when those taunting lips had played with hers.

When he released her, she smiled tremulously and stepped back, pretending it had been no big deal. She vaguely heard Rafael ask everyone to be seated. When she turned to find a chair, she saw Lena peering at her thoughtfully.

Ramón seated himself directly across the table from her, while Lena plopped herself to his left and Esperanza meekly took the chair to his right.

As soon as they were all seated, Lena began asking him a barrage of questions. By the time they ordered their dinner and it arrived, Consuelo had finished her second drink. Almost everyone had ordered beef or chicken fajitas as well as *chilies reyenos* and enchiladas with rice and beans.

Meanwhile, Consuelo tried to think of some excuse to leave. Lena had commandeered Ramón's attention and was driving her crazy with all her hand talking. Her hands moved in quick birdlike gestures, her long, scarlet-colored nails like talons closing in for the kill.

A few minutes later, Lena asked Ramón, "If you don't mind me asking, what are you planning to build on your property?"

"I don't mind you asking," he replied easily, setting down his fork. "I've begun plans to build a strip mall."

Lena looked at him quizzically. "Will you tear down Salvador's building, then?"

Ramón shook his head. "I'm using it as my office. Actually, I'm building on his other property, across the street."

For once, Lena was speechless. She stared at him openmouthed, then managed to croak out, "But that's where the shrine is."

He gave a careless shrug. "Yes."

Josie spoke up. "What will happen to the tree?"

"It's just a tree. It'll have to go."

"Go where?" Esperanza asked.

He started to reply, but Consuelo cut him off. "Surely seven years hasn't dulled your memory, Ramón. The Annual Shrine Festival is less than two months away. We need that shrine." She might be his guest, but this was her establishment, and she refused to sit meekly in the background.

He stared at her. "*We*, Consuelo? I thought only single women were allowed to participate in the ritual."

Her chin rose a notch. "I've never participated, and it isn't a ritual. It's a celebration, and I'm speaking for a lot of people in this town. Why can't the tree stay?"

He leaned back, a cool challenge in his eyes.

"It's too near the middle of the property. Some of the trees will have to go in order to accommodate the buildings. It's unfortunate but necessary."

"And when do you propose to do that?" Now she understood why he'd invited her here. He'd set her up. He'd set them all up. He'd known Lena would bring up the subject. And he'd wanted to see her reaction. Payback time?

"I plan to start leveling the land in a week or two."

Lena made one last effort. "Salvador loved that shrine. He promised the shrine would stay there forever."

Ramón nodded. "That might be, but he's not around to argue the point. And yes, it's unfortunate he and his family were killed and that his only living heir decided to sell it, but it happens to be an ideal location for what I want." His eyes challenged Consuelo.

Forcing herself to remain cordial, she stood and excused herself. "I'll be right back," she told everyone.

She rushed to the kitchen, thankful Luna and Juana were there.

"Quick, think of something to get me out of there. I can't go through with this."

"What happened?" Luna's concern was obvious.

Consuelo took a deep breath and let it out. "I can't talk about it right now. I'm just . . . uncomfortable."

"Something happened. I know you; you wouldn't have left without a good reason."

"I'll tell them I'm ill."

Luna's eyes widened. "No! You can't tell them you're ill."

"Why not?"

"You look too healthy. Ramón would never believe you. Let me think."

"Well, think quick."

Luna thought for a moment before pushing Consuelo toward the door. "Okay, but you'd better go back until I can come up with something."

By the time Consuelo returned to the table, they were all discussing some recent movie they'd seen. Consuelo picked up her margarita and took a sip. The glass was empty, so she picked at her food instead until finally she pushed her plate to one side.

Ten minutes later, Consuelo had given up on Luna coming up with a plausible excuse for her to leave. The margaritas had made her feel mellow, so she no longer kept vigil on the doorway. She was chatting amiably with Josie and didn't hear Luna enter the room and call her name.

Finally, Luna's voice rang out clearly. "Ah, Consuelo, your date is here."

Her what? Consuelo stared at her sister as though she'd lost her mind, then it dawned on her that it must be a ruse intended for her to leave. Good girl.

"Well, it's been nice, everyone." She started to rise, but Ramón's husky voice stopped her.

"Why don't we pull up another chair for your date?"

Consuelo's brows drew together. "We have other plans, and I'm sure he's already eaten."

"Why don't you ask him?" Ramón said.

"I can't. He's probably waiting right outside the door."

"No, he's not," Ramón countered, glancing toward the doorway.

Consuelo jerked her head toward the door. Luna was gone, and in her place stood a teenager about eighteen years old.

"How long did you want me to wait?" the young man asked.

Consuelo groaned inwardly, wanting to murder her sister. She managed a smile. "I'd better go, but thank you, Ramón, for the dinner invitation. It was . . . interesting."

Ramón spoke directly to the young man. "Are you sure you can't join us? The food is excellent."

"Well, ah . . ."

Consuelo rushed to the door. "We'd better go." She grabbed the young man's arm and waved good-bye.

Just as they stepped outside the room, she heard Ben shout, "You'd better have him home by twelve."

No one laughed. They were probably still in shock, Consuelo thought, as she escorted her *date* outside.

In the parking lot, she turned to face him. "What's your name?"

"Hector."

"Okay, Hector. First, I want to apologize. I didn't know Luna had called you."

"She sounded pretty desperate."

"Well, you did fine. Where's your car?"

"Over there. Where do you want to go?"

"Drive me around to the back."

A few minutes later, Consuelo entered the kitchen and glared at Luna, who managed a sheepish smile.

"You told me to think up something quick. It was the best I could do in such a short time."

Consuelo gritted her teeth. "I am so humiliated."

Just then, Enrique burst through the door, and both women jumped. "Thought you'd like to know that Ramón is on his way in here."

Cosuelo and Luna exchanged worried glances.

"Here?" both sisters shrieked in unison. Consuelo uttered an unladylike oath as she rushed into the broom closet. What if he'd seen Hector drive her around to the back? *What if he suspects I'm in here?* Mortified, she leaned against the door to listen.

"Hi, Ramón. Is everything all right?" Luna asked.

Ramón smiled politely and nodded a greeting to Juana, who nodded back and continued to make tortillas.

He held up a woman's jacket. "Consuelo left this behind. Would you see that she gets it?"

"Of course. Thank you."

"By the way, who was the young man?"

Luna gave him an innocent smile. "His name is Hector Samuels. Actually, he's older than he looks. His father owns a software company, and Hector is a computer genius."

Ramón appeared thoughtful. "I see. Well, tell her I'm sorry she couldn't stay."

Consuelo still had her ear plastered to the door when someone opened it, and she jumped. When she stepped out, Luna was grinning from ear to ear.

"Did you hear? He's jealous."

Consuelo frowned. "Of that . . . that child? *Por Dios,* Luna, he was probably wondering if I'd taken leave of my senses."

"I don't think so, Sis."

Consuelo grabbed her jacket. "Of course, you're such an expert on men."

"I know enough to recognize interest."

"Well, you're wrong." Wanting to change the subject, she asked, "Hector's father owns a software company?"

"Not exactly. He's more of a manager," Luna replied rather timidly, which made Consuelo more suspicious.

"What exactly does Hector the computer genius do for a living?"

"He sells software."

Consuelo froze in the act of donning her jacket. "He's a salesman?"

"At Toys 'R' Us."

Consuelo groaned. "I'm going to bed. You and Juana lock up."

Four

Twenty women gathered in the church court-yard right after nine o'clock mass to discuss the latest turn of events.

Everyone pretty much agreed that tearing down the shrine had to be about the worse thing to happen in Sandera since Sarah Gonzalez had given up her faith, which was a huge shock considering that Sarah had constantly gone around talking to God.

One of her neighbors muttered that Sarah had probably tired herself out and suffered burnout. Either that or she had a secret she wasn't telling anyone.

Apolonia Saldana wondered if Sarah was tormented from an affair that had turned sour just like her face. No one agreed or disagreed.

Lidia Sanchez finally suggested they not waste another precious moment on Sarah's love life when they had a shrine to save.

"But what can we do?" someone asked.

"We need to talk him out of it, that's what."

"I think he's pretty much made up his mind."

"We have to think of something and quick."

"Ladies, one at a time, please," shouted Lidia.

"I think we all agree that we need *un emisario*—a representative who will discuss the situation calmly and rationally with Ramón. He has to know how serious the situation is."

Calmly and rationally? Buena suerte, thought Consuelo, who almost laughed out loud. That is, until she noticed all eyes had turned in her direction.

Leaning against the courtyard fountain, she glanced over her shoulder to see if they were looking at someone else. They weren't, and she straightened. "Oh, no, you don't."

Lidia's twin sister, Loretta, added her two cents. "But, Consuelo, you two were close friends."

"That was a long time ago."

Lidia plowed on. "Most of us have children and husbands and households to take care of. We can't spare the time."

"And I can?"

"Well, he *is* just across the street, Connie," offered Luna.

Consuelo stared at her sister, willing her to be quiet.

Lena Morales had remained silent throughout the discussion, which was a miracle in itself, sitting ramrod straight in the way she'd been taught as a child. Now, her body suddenly shifted forward. "He's having dinner at our home on Thursday. Perhaps we can persuade him to change his mind."

Those women who had unmarried daughters stared at Lena's offspring, sizing her up as competition.

Lidia smiled. "Excellent idea, Lena. You can serve as our backup." Her attention snapped back to Consuelo. "But we still need you to speak on our behalf."

Consuelo frowned. "I don't think that's a good idea."

Luna spoke up again. "You know him better than most of us, Consuelo."

Consuelo ignored her sister. "I don't think Ramón is going to sink money into a project and then calmly walk away."

Lidia was dauntless in her pursuit. "I'm sure you'll think of something. Ladies, what do you think?"

"Wait a minute," Consuelo said.

"I propose we elect Consuelo to be our spokesperson in this matter," declared Apolonia excitedly.

"I second it!" Luna shouted.

"Luna, don't you have to be somewhere else?" Consuelo asked.

"I don't go to work for you until two o'clock, remember?"

Consuelo was getting a bad feeling about this. These women didn't understand that she was the last person Ramón would listen to. Last night, she'd seen his shrewd eyes pin her when he'd mentioned his plans for the property *and* the shrine. He'd wanted to see her reaction, had probably planned it down to the last crummy detail. *Peace treaty, my foot!* He'd deliberately goaded her.

Lidia clutched her large, square purse close to

her midriff with both her tiny wrists. "You may handle the situation any way you see fit. As far as we're concerned, the end justifies the means."

In Consuelo's mind, that meant they were giving her carte blanche to do anything she had to in order to save their beloved shrine. She stared into the sea of faces as they waited for her to say something, and in their eyes the trust showed. She looked away. She didn't want to be anybody's hope.

"All I can do is try," she said honestly.

"That's all we ask. *Andele pues y buena suerte,*" Lidia said as she slapped her purse against her thigh.

Which meant the meeting was adjourned.

As Lidia Sanchez had pointed out so succinctly, there was a lot to do and not a whole lot of time left in which to do it.

Maybe if she reminded Ramón how important, how necessary the shrine was to these people, he would understand. Without it, there would be no celebration.

At his desk, Ramón slouched in his chair and peered through the venetian blinds of his window, lazily surveying the woman walking toward him. As she came closer, he noticed the determination in her stride and in the set of her chin. Consuelo Rodriquez walked like a woman with a purpose.

He watched as a sudden gust of wind picked up her hair and she reached up to push it away from her face. The bloodred dress emphasized the soft curves of her body. His gaze lowered to a pair of very shapely legs.

He grabbed a magazine off his desk just before she opened the door.

As soon as she entered, he glanced up and smiled. "Hello, Connie. What brings you here on this beautiful Monday evening?" He studied her a moment. "Let me guess. You're the one who's been recruited to talk me out of it."

"How did you know?"

"Why else would you be here?"

He'd said the words casually, but his meaning was unmistakable. She glanced around the room. "You've changed the place," she said, noticing a drop cloth and several paint cans lined up against the far wall.

Ramón stood up, towering over her. "Yeah. Just a little paint here and there, and I got rid of the counter and a few other things."

Even though Consuelo preferred bold colors, she couldn't help but note that the neutral shades of the room suited him. Outlined against the honey beige wall, he looked breathtakingly masculine. He wore a green T-shirt that matched the color of his eyes and emphasized the muscles of his chest, and a pair of faded, work-worn jeans. His cowboy boots were dusty, and she wondered where he'd been today. She glanced at his chest again. It was easy to recall how she'd lain in the safety of those arms and pressed her cheek against his shoulder. She swallowed and looked toward the stairs that led to a second floor.

"Would you like to see the second floor?"

"Sure," she said and followed him up the stairs.

The first thing she noticed was a large living room. The second was how close he stood to her, making her painfully aware that their shoulders almost touched.

"No furniture yet. I took down a wall to make this room larger. I didn't need two bedrooms, so I did the same thing with the bedroom," he said, pointing toward one of the rooms.

Consuelo was half afraid he'd invite her to see his bedroom, so she walked over to the living room window and forced herself not to think about the past or what they'd meant to each other. There was something too personal, too intimate, about standing in this room alone with him. She told herself the reason she felt so skittish around him was because she wasn't used to seeing him.

She crossed her arms in front of her chest and looked out the window. "Interesting view," she said and smiled, then almost jumped when she turned and found him so close, as she hadn't heard him walk up behind her.

"Yeah, how about that?" he replied, returning her smile.

She returned her attention to the view and noticed that from where she stood, if her French doors were open in her apartment, he'd be able to see directly into her bedroom. The windows were in direct line with each other.

She deliberately kept her back to him. "I'm so used to seeing this place as Salvador's shoe repair

store, I can't believe I won't be seeing him anymore," she said with a tinge of regret. "He was
happy here. I remember when he added this second floor so his family could be close. In fact, I
got the idea from him."

"Yes, they were close . . . even died together."

She nodded. "He always intended for his business and property to go to one of his children. Who
could've known a distant cousin would inherit."

"Or that he would sell it to me."

She turned to look at him, but he didn't so much
as flicker an eyelash to reveal what he was thinking.
She knew it wasn't going to be easy, but she wanted
him to understand. "The reason Salvador wanted
one of his children to have it is because he knew
they would keep it in the family and hand it down
to their heirs. You can't have been gone that long
as to forget that these people worship that shrine."

There, she'd thrown it out into the open.

"Things change, Connie. Sometimes we may
not like it, but those are the facts of life. They'll
get over it."

She couldn't let it pass. "Doesn't it bother you
that you'll be hurting some of the people who
were friends with your father?"

He looked out the window toward her balcony.
"Sentimentality doesn't belong in a business ven-
ture. You of all people should know that."

She'd known he wouldn't budge. To him, the
tree was merely an obstacle to getting what he
wanted.

"Ramón, what made you buy this property to
begin with? I mean, I know of a few other good

pieces of land that are for sale with fewer trees on them."

"I wanted this one," he said matter-of-factly.

"But why?"

"Do I have to have a reason? It was on the market, it's toward the end of town, and it suits my needs."

Consuelo tried not to look in the direction of his bedroom and glanced down at her watch instead. "I'd better go. Thanks for the tour," she said flatly.

"Are you giving up that easily?"

"Is your mind made up?"

"Yep."

She shrugged a delicate shoulder. "Then that's that. There's nothing else to say."

"So this was your best shot?" he asked as he escorted her to the door.

Consuelo nodded.

"If you say so." He didn't look convinced as he watched her disappear out the door.

When she was gone, Ramón sat down again. He wasn't fooled into believing that she'd really given up. There were few men he trusted, and even fewer women. He'd already tasted those beautiful lying lips, and had no intention of falling into her trap ever again. However, as long as he kept those rules in mind, there was no reason why he couldn't have a little fun with her, tease her now and then. He knew her well enough to sense that there was something mighty powerful brewing inside Consuelo Rodriquez.

* * *

As Consuelo stepped out of Ramón's office, she saw the last faint color of day and realized she'd just wasted her day off. Her visit with Ramón had been nothing but a futile waste of energy. She had told the committee of women that she'd do what she could. And she had. Her responsibility ended here.

She was about to cross the street when she happened to glance toward the shrine. A woman and a young boy of about six sat on the bench beside the tree. She realized it was Nina Vasquez. Consuelo switched direction and headed toward them.

She slowed down her pace before she reached them and came to a halt several yards away. Deep in prayer, Nina had her eyes closed, while her son kept looking down at the ground. They'd eaten at her restaurant occasionally, and Consuelo had noticed lately she and her son came in alone. Consuelo's heart constricted. Their heads were together, and the moment looked too personal to interrupt. Was Nina having marital problems? Did she pray for the return of her husband?

Somewhere from several streets away, a siren wailed, and she hoped it was no one she knew. Consuelo stood there a moment longer, wondering how she could make a hasty exit without being spotted. The faces of Lidia Sanchez and the other women floated before her eyes. She had failed them. Worse, she didn't know what else to do. What would it take for Ramón to change his mind?

She didn't know the answer, but she had to find out.

*   *   *

A dark eyebrow rose quizzically when Ramón noticed the same familiar blur of red outside his window. He watched, amused, as Consuelo approached his door again. Only now, the determined glint in her eyes had been replaced by unwavering resolution. Joan of Arc couldn't have looked any more indomitable.

She stepped into the office and spread both palms down on his desk. "I need to talk to you."

"Again? This must be my lucky day."

"Would you stand up, please?"

He feigned surprise. "That depends. Are you going to hurt me?"

She almost smiled. "I'm in no mood for jokes, Ramón. I'd like you to come with me. Please."

He stood and looked down at her. "Well, since you said it so nicely, I'll go. It must be important for you to come back so quickly. Or do I dare hope that you're here for some other reason?"

"No other reason," she said, moving away from him.

The corners of his eyes crinkled in amusement. "And if I had said no, you'd probably keep pestering me, wouldn't you."

"You know me too well." Against her better judgment, she returned his smile.

He moved closer and she cleared her throat. "Come on, it will only take a moment."

As they made their way toward the shrine, neither of them spoke. By the time they reached the site, Consuelo was disappointed to find that Nina had already left.

Consuelo stood there, her insecurities rising

like the rancid aftertaste of a bad meal, but she plowed right through them.

"A woman and her child just left this site, and I wish you could've been here to see them, Ramón. She was praying. Doesn't that mean something to you? Have you been gone so long that you don't remember what it's like to believe in something?"

He shook his head. "There's a church for things like that. Besides, have you thought of what my coming here will do for this town? The construction alone will bring extra jobs and money to these people, not to mention new businesses."

"Yes, it will bring jobs, but you'll also be taking away their faith, the beliefs they've held on to all their lives."

He grabbed her shoulders and turned her around to face the object of their argument. "Look at it. It's just a tree, for Christ's sake."

"Only because that's all *you* see."

He sighed and let her go. "Look, it isn't personal," he assured her. "It's business. Besides, think of all the water the city will save by not having to water the tree."

Infuriated by his remark, Consuelo's eyes narrowed to dangerous slits. "It isn't personal? Then you might want to explain that to Lupe Salazar, who prayed right here on this spot for her husband to return home from the war after he'd been missing in action for several years. They were reunited. Or to Lucy Longoria, who prayed to conceive a child after trying for seven years—"

"I thought this tree was only for single women looking for husbands."

"Soul mates. But that's only part of it. It's also about people—whether lovers or husbands or sweethearts—being reunited."

Consuelo would have continued, but Ramón's strong arms grabbed her and pulled her close fast. His mouth came down in a punishing kiss that took her by surprise. She struggled to push him away. She could feel the heat of his body as her heart pounded against his chest. Finally, she went limp and his mouth relaxed, becoming more gentle and exploring. He'd always had the power to make her go weak with a mere touch. Now, after so long without him, her senses came alive and she returned his kiss.

With some effort, he released her. "I should apologize, but I'm not going to." There was a trace of irritation in his voice. "It seemed the only way I could shut you up."

She opened her mouth to speak, but something in her peripheral vision caught her attention.

"Oh, no," she cried.

He glanced over to see what had upset her. A short distance away, Berta Leal stood watching them, her face a study of deep wrinkles and her dark eyes several shades of curious.

Berta quickly averted her gaze and continued on her way.

"See what you've done? By tomorrow, everyone in town will know you kissed me under this tree. That was Berta, and she's been talking to Lena. Ramón, you creep, you knew she was there."

"No, I didn't."

She ignored him. "And to make matters worse, Berta caught us doing this eight years ago."

For an instant the corners of his mouth lifted in a smile as he remembered the event, but it was quickly wiped away.

"You're incorrigible. What am I going to do?"

"Tell her we're testing the tree theory?"

Trying to hang on to her patience, she cried, "Why can't you listen? Why can't you at least let the town enjoy their celebration? Would that be so terrible?"

He held up a hand. "Time is money. In the first place, I don't believe in soul mates, and I don't believe in miracles. All those so-called miracles you mentioned would've happened anyway, with or without a shrine. The tree is going."

Consuelo's hackles rose. "You may not believe in this shrine, but if you have any ideas about Esperanza, don't forget that Berta will tell Lena and Lena will tell her daughter."

He regarded her for a moment. "I think I'm missing something here. Should this be bothering me?" He noted the tiny lines feathering the corners of her beautiful dark eyes—eyes that still had the power to make him feel something. Whenever she looked at him like she did now, he felt as though someone had just hit him in the gut with a padded fist. His glance fell to her mouth. For a moment, staring at that mouth made him weak—weak enough to reach out and pull her to him again. But he resisted the impulse.

The warmth went out of his gaze so quickly that Consuelo thought she must have imagined it. She bit back her disappointment. "I'm tired of this conversation," she spouted. "I thought I could appeal to your sense of fairness and goodness, but I might as well be talking to the tree."

"You're right. And don't try to con me, because it won't work."

She lifted her chin a notch and gave him her most frigid smile. "This tree isn't going anywhere. I haven't even begun to fight yet."

He tilted his head back and laughed.

Pushing past him, she shouted over her shoulder, "Go to hell!"

"You'd better watch your mouth. You're on sacred ground." He was still grinning when she reached the other side of the street.

No doubt about it, he recognized a challenge when he saw one.

Five

The room was dimly lit by two half-burned candles in the shape of apples, their subtle aroma floating in the air.

She stood before her kitchen counter, gazing into a bowl half filled with flour. Slipping her hands into the bowl, she closed her eyes. Not from weariness, but because of the man standing behind her, whose nude body pressed lightly against her own.

On the counter to her right, peaches and strawberries released an enticing scent that caused her to salivate, and she almost reached for one of the strawberries. Instead, she grabbed a cup of water, poured some into the bowl, and began kneading the dough, all the while aware of the man's hands traveling steadily up her spine.

His fingers continued their lazy path along her shoulders, down her arms, to the swelling fullness of her breasts. He cupped the ripe, firm flesh, circling the nipples with his thumbs. She moaned softly, enjoying the feel of those fingers working magic on her skin. His hands moved to join hers in the bowl, caressing and entwining, both now sharing the soft texture of the dough.

His hands, sticky with dough, resumed their assault on her nipples, leaving a trail of dough along the way. All the while, she could feel his erection pressed against

*her from behind. Libidinous pleasure swept through her
body, her breasts, causing her body to throb with need.*

"Please," she pleaded.

He turned her to face him.

"Please, what?" He smiled.

"Make love to me, Ramón."

"Not quite yet, querida." *He reached over, picked up
a strawberry, bit into it and then offered her the rest by
gently placing it in her mouth.*

*One of the candles flickered dangerously, threatening
to die out, and she could see the flame reflected in his
green eyes. Suddenly, his hands wrapped around her
waist and he lifted her to sit on the counter, then gently
nudged her thighs open so he could settle himself more
comfortably against her.*

She opened herself willingly, trustingly.

*His mouth lowered to hers and devoured her while his
hands touched her everywhere. His kiss deepened, inviting her tongue to mate with his. He tasted of strawberries and wine and male desire.*

*Her arms wound around his neck, clutching him
closer, wanting, needing him inside her. He responded to
her ardor by touching her in her most private place,
readying her for his entry. His hardness searched, then
slowly began to enter her.*

*Clutching him tighter, she moaned into his mouth,
but suddenly found herself clutching thin air, for he was
disappearing before her eyes. Her body craved release but
he was fading. . . .*

"Noooo!" Consuelo cried, burrowing deeper
under the covers. Turning on her side, she drew

her knees up to her chest, cursing the dream gods for not letting her and Ramón finish what they'd started.

Six years of celibacy had left her body throbbing with unfulfilled desire, and she closed her eyes trying to recapture the dream. But it was gone, and no amount of wishful thinking would bring it back.

"What's wrong?" Luna cried out as she came running into the room.

"I . . . nothing. I was just having a bad dream," she lied. It had been a really good dream . . . or would've been, had she been able to finish it.

Luna sighed in relief. "For a moment, I thought you were being attacked. You screamed loud enough to wake the dead."

"I'm sorry. I didn't mean to wake you."

"That's all right. I had to get up anyway. Can I get you some water or something?"

Consuelo moved to a sitting position and leaned against the headboard. "No, thanks."

"You've been awfully quiet the last couple of days. You want to talk about it?"

"It's nothing. Probably PMS." She smiled.

Luna returned the smile, although she wasn't fooled. "You don't have to pretend, you know. Not with me."

"Have you developed some psychic talent that I'm not aware of?"

Luna shrugged. "When it comes to you, sometimes I think I have."

Consuelo stared at her sister, moved by her

words. She reached out and touched her hand. "I feel the same way about you."

"Then tell me what's wrong."

Consuelo folded her hands in her lap and studied them, strangely comparing them with Ramón's. There *was* no comparison; both of hers would have fit in one of his. "Have you ever been in love, Luna?"

Luna was candid, as always. "No, I can't say that I've ever experienced that deep, abiding love that a lot of people talk about. Actually, I don't even think I like men."

"That's because the ones you date let you boss them around. You need someone who'll bring you down a peg or two, that's all. Maybe you should visit the shrine this year," Consuelo said in a half-mocking tone.

"Have you heard something I haven't? I thought the shrine was history."

Consuelo sighed. "Who knows? Maybe something will happen to make Ramón change his mind."

"You mean a miracle? Last I heard, his mind was pretty much set on killing the tree."

Consuelo nodded.

"Oh, by the way, I found a home for Sampson." They had decided on the kitten's name together.

"Oh? Anyone I know?"

"Yeah. Mom."

Surprise lit Consuelo's features.

"Actually," Luna continued, "Sampson is technically mine, but she'll feed and bathe him."

Consuelo laughed. "At least he'll stay in the

family." She was delighted with the news. She'd lived in fear that the kitten might happen out onto the balcony and fall off.

Consuelo started to climb out of bed, then changed her mind. She paused and lowered her voice. "Luna, do you dream much?"

"Yeah, sure, once in a while."

"Do you dream"—Consuelo's face flamed as she spoke—"erotic dreams?"

Luna's dark eyebrow arched. "By erotic do you mean 'you Tarzan, me Jane' or whips and chains?"

"I mean do you ever dream of food?"

Luna looked at her sister incredulously for a moment, then smiled. "I think I've got to hear this."

Consuelo cleared her throat. "I've been having these dreams about Ramón . . . and food. In one, I rolled him up in a tortilla and almost ate him. I would've wolfed him down, but Juana woke me up. In another dream, I'm mixing flour and water and I'm craving strawberries. Lots of them."

"Is that all? I thought you said you'd dreamed of Ramón?"

"Yes, we almost made love on the counter."

"Our counter?"

"Yes. It's driving me crazy. There's always so much food around, I swear I'm starting to gain weight."

"Maybe if you go to bed with him, the dreams will stop."

Consuelo had no intention of going to bed with Ramón, and she could safely bet that he felt the same way. "I don't intend to find out if you're right. Now scat, I've got to get up. My world awaits."

Later, after Consuelo had showered and sat brushing her hair, she agonized over why she was having such dreams about Ramón.

She had no doubt that he'd turned into a beast. Thank God she'd been spared from making a terrible mistake. The young man that Ramón had been seven years ago never would have treated her the way he had last night. The kiss meant nothing to either one of them, and she refused to let herself think otherwise. She vowed not to let him get to her.

If she'd been harboring any illusions that he might've returned home to see her, they were certainly gone now. She suspected he'd come here for revenge. Why else would he return to town out of the blue when he'd been doing so well in Chicago?

But how could she look at him now and not remember some of the happiest times of her life? In her darkest hours and saddest fears, Ramón's memory had been the one she'd clung to the most. He'd been her world.

And for what? He hated her now.

For a moment, tears threatened to spill, but she wouldn't cry. She'd already shed too many.

He was going to be trouble. She'd known it from the first time he'd appeared from the shadows, waiting to speak to her. Her mind wandered to the evening before, when he'd kissed her under the tree, and she wondered how long it would take Berta to spread the news.

Setting the brush down, she noticed the flyer lying near the edge of the table, and picked it up. Ramón's renovation project for Lupe Espinoza's home would take place on Saturday. Enrique had been singing his praises all week. She wondered how he could be so callous one moment and then turn around and do something so wonderful.

With a tight expression, she pitched the flyer into the wastepaper basket beside her vanity and stood up. She had better things to do with her time than to spend it reliving the past.

Ramón sagged on the edge of his bed and blinked, trying to rub the sleep out of his eyes.

Damn it, he'd dreamed of her again, of her waiting mouth and the rosy tips of her breasts, and her hot, eager body. The ringing of the phone had interrupted their session or he'd be washing the sheets right now.

And why in the hell was he dreaming about her anyway? During his four-year stint in the service, and later when he'd decided to move to Chicago, after facing the fact that she would never be his, he had cultivated the ability to block her out of his mind. Experience had taught him to focus all his energies onto one goal at a time. Right now, the building project was his main priority, and Consuelo Rodriquez was just a minor inconvenience.

But he knew her well enough to know she wouldn't give up.

By the time he showered, dressed, and headed straight for the kitchen, his mood had gone from bad to worse.

Raul took one look at his brother and snorted in disgust. "It must be a damn curse," he muttered. "First it was Rafael who turned stubborn and bullheaded and moped around here until Josie tamed him. Now you," he accused. "I don't know what the hell's eating you, *hermano,* but I don't intend to go through this merry-go-round twice, so you'd better do something about it quick. My patience is wearing thin."

Ramón grabbed a cup from a cabinet, poured himself some coffee from the coffeepot on the stove, and then joined Raul at the table. "I've got a couple of things on my mind," he said as he sipped his coffee. "And as soon as my furniture arrives, I'll be staying in town."

"You know you're welcome to stay here for as long as you like. Hell, it's your home, too. And if I've overstepped my bounds, then tell me. But if I'm right and you *do* have women problems, then I suggest you nip them in the bud, 'cause there's nothing worse than a lovesick Santos man running around loose. Now, pass the cream."

Ramón stared at his brother and broke into his first genuine grin since his return home. "Now that you've said your piece, brother, let's get the hell out of here and go to El Paso to have some fun."

"Now you're talking," replied Raul. "I understand there are some pretty señoritas just waiting for us."

"Hell, I'm game," Ramón said as he took his wallet out and checked it. "But first I'd better go to the bank. I'll meet you back here in an hour."

He set the wallet on the table and got up to go pour himself another cup of coffee. When he returned, he picked up his wallet and headed out the door, coffee mug in hand.

Ramón was standing in the bank lobby twenty-five minutes later when, as he was slipping the cash into his wallet, he saw two condoms tucked haphazardly inside. For a moment he wondered how they got there, then it dawned on him that Raul must've put them there when he'd gotten up to get his second cup of coffee. He threw his head back and laughed, scaring a bystander in the bank.

As it turned out, it being the middle of the week, there weren't many señoritas to woo. And to make matters worse, they ran into a rainstorm on the way home. By the time they returned in the wee hours of the morning, all they'd gotten for their efforts were upset stomachs and hangovers.

Consuelo stood awkwardly on Lupe Espinoza's front lawn with both her hands shoved into the back pockets of her worn jeans. She watched with curious fascination the amount of activity going on in front of her. At least twenty people had turned out to help today.

She spotted Ramón standing close to the porch speaking to Enrique. She was apprehensive about approaching him, so she waited for him to glance her way as she shifted her weight from one foot to the other.

Enrique was the first to see her. His face creased into a smile and he waved hello. She waved back.

Something shifted in the stormy depths of Ramón's eyes as he made his way toward her.

"What are you doing here?"

Consuelo handed him the flyer. "You asked for volunteers, didn't you?"

He placed one hand on his hip and stood in that arrogant stance she was beginning to dislike so much. "I assumed since it was Saturday, you wouldn't be able to leave the restaurant."

She slipped past him. "I may own a business, Ramón, but I *do* manage to have a life. So are you going to show me what you want me to do?" There was a pause. "Unless you're turning down extra help?"

He studied the stubborn tilt of her chin. "Of course not. Come on, I'll put you to work."

He led her over to where Enrique knelt on the ground, relieving a window frame of its dirt, grime, and old paint.

"You can help Enrique get the old paint off those windows. We'll give them a fresh coat of paint later."

She grabbed the sander off the ground and began work. A moment later, she was interrupted by a shout from the roof. She glanced up to see Rafael and Raul smiling and waving. In the midst of returning their wave, a shadow crossed her path and she looked up into the uncompromising features of Ramón. She quietly went back to work.

She'd gotten through half a window when someone tapped her on the shoulder. "Hey, Sis, if I had known you wanted to come today, I would've given you a ride."

Consuelo's surpise was evident. "I thought you'd made other plans today."

"Yeah, I did and he's here," she said, motioning over her shoulder.

Consuelo nodded a greeting to Marcus. Or was it Mario? She couldn't keep up with Luna's friends.

"Since I'm not working this weekend, I thought it would be cool to help."

"Of course it's all right. I'm glad you decided to work at the restaurant for the next couple of weeks," Consuelo said as she returned to her task.

"Me too. Where's your car? I don't see it."

"I jogged part of the way and walked the rest."

"Well, if you need a ride home, let us know," Luna said as she walked away with her boyfriend in tow.

Consuelo had just finished her third window and stopped to rest. Glancing toward the house, she wondered if Lupe was home. She hadn't seen the elderly woman in a long time.

Besides Rafael and Raul, who were still repairing the roof, she noticed other familiar faces, including Ignacio Flores; Juan Sanchez, Lidia's husband; and Ben Solis, Ramón's cousin. Some were power-washing the house, others were mowing the backyard and hauling off old roofing and other materials. She switched her attention to Ramón. He was repairing the porch and she watched, fascinated, as he sawed a board in half, sanded the edges, and then ran his fingers over the smooth wood. His denim jeans were tight and faded and his shirt was open to the waist, exposing a flat stomach and glistening skin. She knew what that skin would feel like. Smooth and lean and warm.

But it was his hands that drew her. She had always loved his hands. They were large and strong, his fingers long and blunt. She resisted the urge to reach out and touch them. How many boards had those hands touched? How many women had they caressed?

Consuelo looked away. She had no business ogling the man and she'd best remember that. She glanced at the house again and thought of Lupe. The paint had peeled and the porch had begun to rot and crumble. Consuelo recalled that Lupe had been born here.

Lupe was very special to her. She'd been Consuelo's fifth-grade teacher, and had taken her to task on several occasions for skipping school and failing math. One day, Lupe had handed Consuelo her home address and ordered the child to be at her house at six sharp. "And be prompt," she'd said in that no-nonsense voice of hers.

That had been the beginning of Consuelo's weekly tutoring sessions, where she'd gotten dinner and a math lesson. Consuelo could almost hear her voice. "All right, Consuelo, Pepe Longoria sold eight of his pigs today. That leaves him with twenty. How many do you think he had to begin with?"

Consuelo's hands would rest in her lap as she counted quickly on her fingers. "Twenty-eight. He had twenty-eight."

"Next time I expect you to do it quicker. But use your mind, not your fingers, *comprendes*?"

And that's how Consuelo learned her math. Lupe's tutoring extended to other such examples as Juan Vargas's cattle, Pepe's pigs (although they kept dwindling), Antonio Zepeda's vast sheep herd, and so on. Consuelo smiled. Not only had she passed math, but she'd grown to love Lupe.

"Am I taking up your valuable time?" a husky voice muttered from behind her.

Consuelo jumped, embarrassed to be caught daydreaming by Ramón. "I was just thinking about something," she said in her defense.

"I need volunteers, not divas. Think on your own time. I don't have time for loafers."

"Loafer?" Consuelo stood and brushed dust and chipped paint off her jeans. She opened her mouth to tell him where he could stick his paintbrush but she choked down the impulse. She could tell by his smirk that he expected her to get angry.

She shrugged. "You're right, Lupe deserves better from me. I've finished the windows, what else do you want me to do?"

He pushed his sunglasses up over his forehead. "You can paint them after lunch. I came to tell you that we're about to eat. There's pizza and drinks over there on that table." He motioned to a spot under a shady tree.

It was on the tip of her tongue to tell him that he could've been a tad more tactful. Instead, she walked to the table and went out of her way to sit as far away from him as possible.

Ramón sat next to Rafael discussing upcoming plans for Rafaela's birthday party, while on the radio Enrique Iglesias belted out that he wanted to be in love with someone. Next, Ricky Martin, as if insulted that he hadn't been picked to sing first, shouted about "La Vida Loca."

A young couple rose and started to dance, trying to emulate Ricky's gyrating hip movements. Laughter, clapping, and a lot of body moving ensued.

Ramón, toe-tapping with the rest, sat on the ground, leaning against an ancient oak. He smiled, enjoying the festive atmosphere. Everyone had been working hard and he was glad they were enjoying themselves.

His eyes strayed toward Consuelo. He knew he'd been rude to her and he felt bad about it, especially since she was doing her best and she *had* volunteered.

His mind wandered to the night under the tree. He shouldn't have kissed her, but she'd looked all fired up to put him in his place. It had been a knee-jerk reaction. He wished those ladies had sent someone else to try and make him change his mind—someone ugly, senile, and flat-chested.

He had to admit, she looked cute in that designer baseball cap, but her thin white T-shirt left nothing to the imagination. A lot of midriff showed.

Now Bryan Adams began to croon "Have You Ever Really Loved a Woman," and he watched, fascinated, as his brother, Raul, grabbed Consuelo and drew her into his arms. As they waltzed around the small area, laughing amiably, he found himself envious.

He stood up to go dump his paper plate and soda can into a garbage sack nearby. He wasn't paying attention, so he didn't notice when the music stopped.

Raul gave one last grandstand gesture and twirled Consuelo into his arms, then playfully twirled her out. Their hands slipped apart and Consuelo twirled right into Ramón.

He grunted as their bodies made contact and reached out to keep her from falling. As his eyes met hers, he noticed two things: his hand on her bare flesh began to tremble, which meant that he was more affected by her than he thought; and the song that had just started playing was one he knew well, the words reminding him of why they could never be friends again.

He glanced down at her and could see by the change in her eyes that she remembered, too.

As though he'd been scalded, he dropped his hand from her waist and turned away.

"Okay, everybody. Time to get back to work," he said a little too gruffly and stalked off, leaving her standing there.

Several hours later, he surveyed the house before him. They had power-washed the dirt, grime, and paint off the house, applied new paint, repaired the roof, and put the new, much safer porch in place. All in all, he was proud of what they had all accomplished.

"Well, that should do it," he told everyone. "Thanks for your contribution. You were a great team."

People started drifting off, although a few of the men planned to return with Ramón tomorrow to finish up minor details.

Consuelo cleaned up her area and returned the sander to Ramón. He thanked her just as Luna and her friend approached Consuelo and asked if she needed a lift home.

Consuelo shook her head. "No, thanks. I'll walk. Besides, I need the exercise."

Ramón gathered his tools and was putting them in his truck when Lupe showed up. Consuelo smiled, happy to see her. They hugged each other and Lupe glanced toward the house. "I figured it would be safe to return home. Oh, my goodness, it looks brand-new," she said proudly. "I'm glad some of you are still here so I can thank you."

"No thanks necessary," Ramón told her. "You've done an excellent job."

Consuelo had learned long ago that praise coming from Lupe was honest, and she was delighted to see her look so happy.

Lupe turned her shrewd gaze on Consuelo. "How is the restaurant business?"

"Fine."

"You've done well for yourself. Do you keep your own books?"

Consuelo nodded. "Yes. Thanks to your tutoring."

Lupe waved her words away. "Bah, you would've done it anyway. You were pretty determined, as I remember."

Lupe turned to Ramón. "And you went on to build houses, I hear."

"For a while. Now I buy and sell land."

She pinned them both with her discerning no-nonsense gaze. "And build malls. Let me see your palm," she ordered Ramón. He complied, and when she was through, she merely grunted.

"Now let me see yours," she said to Consuelo. "No, the other one."

Lifting her right palm, Consuelo wondered what difference it could possibly make which hand she showed Lupe.

The elderly woman studied Consuelo's palm, then let it drop unceremoniously. "Hmmm," was all Ramón and Consuelo got for their effort. Lupe turned and climbed her new steps.

Unable to hide her curiosity, Consuelo called out, "What did you see?"

Lupe turned the doorknob and muttered over her shoulder, "Nothing—just two stubborn fools."

Ramón and Consuelo exchanged glances. "She hasn't changed much, has she?" he said.

"No."

An uncomfortable silence hung between them.

"Do you need a ride home?" he asked.

"No, thanks."

Raul walked up, smiled at her, then turned to Ramón. "Are we still on for tonight?"

Not caring to hear his reply, Consuelo headed home. It was a pretty day, the sun was waning, and a light breeze was coming in off the gulf. The walk would do her good.

With his eyes, Ramón followed her progress along the sidewalk, her hips swaying seductively. The familiar hips he remembered . . . the hips he'd touched.

He climbed into his truck, started the engine, and pulled away from the curb. A moment later, he was almost even with her, but he didn't slow down as he passed her.

His mind wandered to the song. Their song. "I Will Always Love You" sung by Whitney Houston.

She had lied.

Not for the first time, he wondered if it had been such a good idea to come home. Maybe he should just chuck the whole thing and leave again.

Six

The following day another meeting took place after church. Same time, same courtyard, except this time the number of women had doubled.

Consuelo scanned the restless crowd and noticed Berta was among them. Sarah Gonzalez remained suspiciously absent, but no one seemed to care. They were all too worried and with good reason. Rumor had it that Ramón's bulldozer would start leveling his land tomorrow.

The tree stood smack-dab in the middle of the property. No matter which side the machine started leveling from, left or right, eventually it would get to the middle *and* the tree. The tree was much too big to be moved, so the only option was to cut it down.

With a sinking heart, Consuelo shared what information she could. Ramón was being bullheaded. No, he would not yield on the matter. Yes, she'd tried everything she possibly could to talk him out of it, she added, being careful to avoid Berta's pensive stare.

Lena Morales spoke up. "Even Esperanza

couldn't talk him out of it, and she was so gallant about trying."

With a raise of an eyebrow, Berta inquired, "Can we expect to hear wedding bells for those two soon?"

Anyone else would have wilted under the impact of Lena's stare. "It's too early to tell, but we digress from our goal. What is our next step?"

Berta's smile could have been poured on waffles, and Consuelo wondered if she'd told Lena about the kiss she'd shared with Ramón under the tree. Obviously not, from the still hopeful look in Lena's eyes.

"What's our alternative?" Lidia asked. "Do we have any recourse?"

"We could get an injunction," Consuelo announced.

"On what grounds?" Lidia didn't sound too enthused.

"Salvador always promised the tree would remain as a shrine, as a loving tribute to his great great grandparents," Consuelo offered.

"Couldn't that be construed as hearsay since Salvador isn't here to speak on his behalf?" Lidia shook her head sadly. "Who would've ever thought he and his family would die at the same time?" She made the sign of the cross. "And if Ramón can't be persuaded to change his mind, then it all seems futile."

"Surely you're not giving up," Consuelo said as she leaned against the stucco wall. It was the only support she was getting so far and she wondered who Lidia had been talking to. Had someone been prompting her on this? Consuelo's eyes turned stormy and her chin rose a notch. These women had given her a job to do and she wasn't about to give up. At least not yet. "Ladies, let's try another tactic before we throw in the towel."

"Do you really think we have a chance?" Berta asked with a trace of gloom in her voice.

"There's only one way to find out. I've started a petition that we can pass around. It's worth a try. I've also posted one in my restaurant for people to sign. Maybe we can wear him down. Besides, we can't give up now, right?"

"I suppose not," Lidia grumbled, then brightened slightly when the rest of the women muttered words of encouragement.

"I'll get back with you later on this," said Consuelo.

"What about the festival?" Loretta Sanchez asked. "Should we continue planning? I'm in charge of the entertainment."

Similar murmurs echoed from the crowd and with good reason; they didn't want to put in a lot of work if they were going to lose the battle.

Consuelo held up a hand to silence the crowd. "I suggest you go ahead and make plans as usual; however, leave room for possible changes. In other words, try to get a commitment from your people for that date, but keep the purse strings tight until we know something definite."

"That will be difficult to do since they always want a deposit," Loretta added.

"You can always tell them you need approval and the person in charge is out of town." She pinned Loretta with her most positive grin. "If worse comes to worst, I can always sing and dance."

Chuckles and laughter rose from the crowd. Of course, those who knew her well knew she never made idle promises. If the situation warranted it, she was prepared to do whatever necessary to get the job done.

"In fact, I'll get my castanets out of mothballs," she finished on a humorous note.

The meeting adjourned, and while the ladies were not completely convinced about the outcome, they were at least comfortable with the fact that they had picked the right woman to lead their cause.

Leaving the church courtyard, Consuelo walked along the path to the park two blocks away, then cut through to the opposite side. The park was catercorner from the shrine, and she swiftly crossed the street.

On impulse, she walked over and sat on a wooden bench and leaned back. From there, she had a perfect view of Ramón's building and her restaurant. There was no sign of his car, and she wondered if he was at the ranch with Raul. She knew he planned to move into his apartment as soon as his furniture arrived, whenever that would be.

She'd braided her hair today into one long braid, and as a breeze wafted lightly, she tossed the braid over one shoulder and stared blankly across the street at Ramón's concrete building. What if she'd been wrong in giving the women hope? They were counting on her, so what if all of this blew up in her face? She sighed, knowing she didn't have an answer. All she knew was that she had to try.

To the far left, she saw the bulldozer, looking like something dark and evil that had crawled into their lives, just waiting to effect destruction. She stared at it in stony silence.

What would it take for Ramón to change his mind? And would she discover the answer in time? By the time she arrived home, the question still plagued her.

By morning, she stared at her reflection in the oval mirror and gave herself a big grin. Actually, she wasn't sure if her plan would make him change his mind, but it would certainly slow him down.

All the town needed was to keep that tree on the property until the date of the Annual Shrine Festival.

She padded over to the French doors and peeked through the curtains, then frowned in alarm as she spied Ramón in deep conversation with a man she didn't recognize. She opened the doors and stepped onto her balcony. Anxiety increased as she saw the reason for his visit. A backhoe had been delivered and now joined the bulldozer.

Suddenly, he looked up and their eyes met and held, hers accusing and his composed and indiscernible. His gaze dropped to the vee of her nightgown, reminding her she still wore the skimpy gown. She quickly retreated to the safety of her room.

Later, during lunchtime, as she led a couple to their table, she kept thinking about what she planned to do, and of the ramifications if she got caught. During the entire morning, she kept glancing out the window to see if the big beast of a machine had begun its destruction yet.

As it turned out, the bulldozing didn't begin until late afternoon and came to a halt two hours later. At six o'clock, Consuelo went for a jog. On the way back from her two-mile run, she slowed to a trot, glanced toward Ramón's office, and groaned. The furniture van was just pulling up in front of his building, which meant he planned to stay the night. Heading home, she attempted to occupy her mind with something other than the shrine. She had plenty of time to worry.

By midnight, she found herself pacing. At twelve-thirty, she sighed in relief as she heard Luna's familiar footsteps coming in from a date. She waited until her sister had closed her bedroom door before springing into action.

She removed her gown and stepped into a black, long-sleeved jumpsuit that zipped all the way up the front, then slipped her feet into black boots. Standing in the middle of the room, she tried to remember where she'd left her gloves.

She moved quickly to the dresser and opened the drawer, then gave a sigh of relief as she spotted the gloves. The black knit cap lay beside them. She grabbed hat and gloves and headed for the stairs.

Even as she slipped on the cap and stuffed the gloves into a side pocket, she knew she still had time to change her mind.

As she tiptoed down the stairs, Consuelo was half afraid Luna would find her out, so she hurried to the kitchen and squatted down on her haunches to open the lower cabinet door. Spotting what she needed, she grabbed it and was straightening up when she heard a voice behind her. She jerked around, clearly startled.

"*Dios mio*, Luna, don't ever scare me like that again," Consuelo muttered, as she clutched the small bag to her chest.

"Sorry. That doesn't look like a nightgown you're wearing. Any particular reason?"

"I was looking for something."

Luna eyed the small bag in Consuelo's hand. "At one in the morning? In a designer jumpsuit?" She walked over and calmly sat on the edge of the dining table, letting one combat boot swing back and forth. "If you don't mind me asking, Sis, where were you going, and am I invited?"

Concern clawed at her. "It's risky."

"I like it already."

"You'll become an accessory."

"Now you've really piqued my interest. Does it have something to do with Ramón and the shrine?"

"Am I that transparent?"

Luna shrugged. "I know the signs. When you're nervous, you drum those long nails on everything—tables, walls, plates, anything that's near.

Gives you away every time, and you've been drumming all day."

"I see," Consuelo said thoughtfully. "I'll have to watch that the next time I plan a bank heist."

The combat boot kept swinging back and forth.

Consuelo set the bag on the counter and leaned against it. "I'm not sure I have time to explain. Can I catch you later?"

The combat boot now made lazy circles in the air—first clockwise, then switching to counter-clockwise. It was driving Consuelo crazy.

"I see you're thinking about it," Consuelo said flatly.

The swinging stopped and Luna stood up. "I'll be ready in five minutes."

With a sigh of disgust, Consuelo stared at her sister. "Are you always this damn stubborn?"

"It runs in the family," Luna shot over her shoulder as she was running up the stairs.

Consuelo rushed to keep up with her. "Luna, I don't think this is a good idea."

"For me? Or for you?"

"For you."

"Trust me, it is."

Consuelo stopped in midstep. "How can you say that? You don't even know what I'm up to."

"I don't have to, I trust your judgment. Besides, two heads are better than one." Luna already had her blouse off before she'd reached her bedroom. From the doorway, Consuelo stared as her sister slipped on a black, long-sleeved turtleneck top.

Glancing at Consuelo's dark clothing, Luna smiled as she unlaced her boots and tugged them

off so she could slip into a dark pair of camou-
flage fatigues. "This isn't designer, but I bet it'll fit
the bill."

"Rambo would be impressed," Consuelo said,
eyeing the fatigues and combat boots. All Luna
needed to do was smudge dark paint on her face.

"Do you have an extra cap and gloves?" Luna
asked as she retied the laces to her boots.

"Sure, but don't you want to know what I'm
going to do?"

"You can tell me on the way," Luna said as she
shot past her.

Burdened by guilt, but not enough of it to de-
sist from going through with her crazy plan, Consuelo clutched her bundle as she and Luna left
the comfortable security of the building.

The street seemed eerie at that time of the
morning, and the only lighting came from a
streetlight on her side of the street. Consuelo's
heart pumped nervously as they made their way
swiftly to the other side of the road, and as they
stepped onto the property, they crouched low to
the ground, smelling dust and damp earth and
tension. They moved through the shadows, one
agonizing step after another until they reached
the bulldozer—the enemy of the people of
Sandera.

Consuelo prayed Ramón wasn't up at that hour,
although she knew that if he *had* been, he
would've been out there in a flash ready to haul
her carcass off to jail, and crying out in perverse
joy at doing so.

"Here, let me," Luna whispered as she groped

and searched for the gas tank. Fumbling with the lid, she stuck out her hand. "Hand me the stuff."

Consuelo watched as Luna proceeded to break the law, and wondered if she'd be able to hear Ramón's curses from across the street.

They were just about to walk away when headlights appeared in the distance. They froze.

"Get down!" Luna said, grabbing Consuelo's arm and flattening herself on the ground, as close to the bulldozer as she could.

A sheriff's car was patrolling the area. It slowed for a moment, then picked up speed and moved on. Consuelo held her breath for one heart-stopping moment, praying the car wouldn't circle the block.

When it didn't, they rose and hurried across the street. Once they were safely back in Consuelo's kitchen, they gave out a whoop of relief.

"How about a beer?" Luna suggested as she plopped herself on a chair.

Consuelo's hand trembled as she dug two Lone Stars out of the fridge. Might as well, she thought, since she was too wired to sleep.

They sat at the table and drank in companionable silence, and after they finished, they rose and made their way upstairs. In the *sala*, they smiled and hugged each other, too tired to speak.

The two sisters had never felt so close.

Allies in crime.

Companions in peril.

Seven

She'd just donned her bedclothes and now stood next to the small ornate table near the fireplace, where there was food and drink. Lifting a decanter, she started to pour wine into a glass, but a sudden noise caused her to stop and turn.

She jumped in alarm. Just inside her balcony window stood a man whose body was completely enveloped in black clothing, his height and build intimidating.

"A most interesting night, is it not, señorita?"

By candlelight, she saw that his hair was long, past his shoulders, and though he was masked, she could see his eyes were green.

"El Puma," she whispered in horror.

He bowed. "At your service, my lady."

"I suggest you leave the same way you arrived— through the window."

"But we haven't yet had the pleasure of a visit," he said mockingly.

"You snake. How dare you come here."

"Why, I heard in the plaza today that you wished to speak to me. Was that not you?" His teeth gleamed white as he started toward her.

"Halt. I warn you!" Apprehension shot through her

like a bolt of lightning, as she recalled how she'd stood in the square and called him a coward—a foolhardy thing to do.

"You warn me?" His laughter vibrated in the small confines of the room.

She groped for the whip that lay on the chair beside her. She'd practiced only that morning. As the whip uncoiled in her hand, she snapped it with one deft swing and it arced through the air.

He stopped suddenly, glanced down at his arm, and saw she'd drawn blood. For an instant, he stared at her in surprise, but quickly rallied.

"My humblest congratulations. You use the whip almost as expertly as I use a rapier. The only difference is that I have never attacked an unarmed man."

"I warned you. Now leave!"

"But I heard you wished to speak to me."

"Not alone, and certainly not in my bedroom."

"You're quite right. A bedroom should be used for more . . . pleasant interludes."

Her fingers curled tightly around the whip, ready to use it again if necessary. He took another step and again she let the whip crack through the air.

With one sweep of his hand, he grabbed it and jerked her toward him.

They were now chest to chest, his arms around her waist.

"¡Maldito! ¡Hijo de puta!"

"You, my love, have the tongue of a serpent. A mouth as lovely as yours should be put to better use," he said, as his mouth took possession of hers.

She struggled against him to no avail, and slowly he nudged her back until the backs of her knees were touch-

ing her bed. As the kiss deepened, his body gently pressed her down until they were both laying across the bed.

He was upon her, and she felt his hardness. God help her, she wanted him, this enemy of her father's. Yet she would have given herself to him if not for the pounding on her door and her father's voice demanding she open up.

Reluctantly, he pulled away.

"Until we meet again," he whispered, sealing his vow with one last kiss before he disappeared into the night.

The pounding on the door continued.

"Consuelo! Are you in there?"

She woke with a start and glanced around, caught between reality and the dream.

The knocking persisted and she moved to open the door.

Juana stood there, concern in her eyes. It was the first time Consuelo could remember her aunt looking so frazzled.

"What's wrong, Tía?"

Juana pushed past her. "Are you all right? Why was your door locked?"

Consuelo frowned. "I'm sorry, I wasn't aware I'd locked it. I was catching up on some paperwork and I fell asleep."

Relief lit Juana's features, although she still appeared worried. "Again? But it's only eleven in the morning."

"I stayed up late last night reading." Consuelo felt the tiny fib wouldn't matter as long as it made her aunt feel better.

Her aunt visibly relaxed. "I told you that you needed more rest."

"You're right, and I promise to get more rest. Was there something you needed?"

As if suddenly remembering why she was there, Juana said, "Yes. You have a phone call."

Consuelo's heart jumped. *Dios mío,* had someone seen them last night? She swallowed nervously as she imagined being handcuffed in her restaurant in plain sight of her customers.

"Tía," she said a little cautiously, "do you know who it is?"

"It's your mother."

"Oh, how wonderful."

Juana stared at her thoughtfully as she went to pick up the phone.

By noon that day, news had leaked that vandals had damaged the bulldozer and it would be out of commission for a while. How long was anyone's guess, but the important thing was that it wouldn't be causing any destruction for now.

Consequently, when the Women's Shrine Festival Committee called another meeting, it was to praise Consuelo for a job well done. She wondered if they were talking about the petition or the bulldozer.

"Thank you," she said simply. "Let's hope that Ramón comes to his senses."

She went straight from the meeting to Ramón's office. When she entered, he was watering a plant in the corner. He greeted her as he did each time he saw her. With suspicion.

She took the chair directly in front of his desk and got to the point.

"I'm asking you to reconsider. Leave the tree on the premises, Ramón. What can it hurt?"

He came over, sat on the edge of his desk, and crossed his arms over a muscled chest. The black shirt he wore heightened the color of his hair and deepened the green of his eyes.

"Even if I could leave the tree there, it would be an eyesore since I'm leveling everything to the ground. Plans call for a building to be on that site."

She tried another tactic. "Obviously, it's too big to move, and even if it could be, it just wouldn't be the same. It's the ground where the tree grows that's important. It's sacred ground."

"How can you be so sure of that?" his husky voice commanded.

"The legend."

He shrugged. "A story Salvador loved to share with anyone who would listen. He was a storyteller. How do you know he didn't make it all up?"

A trace of annoyance crept into her voice. "Then explain why, after the women visit the shrine on the day of the festival, they meet their sweethearts or husbands within the year?"

"Pure coincidence," he scoffed. "Who knows, maybe they were desperate enough to grab the first guy who approached them."

"Faith moves mountains, Ramón. What happened to yours?" She tried not to let her eyes stray to the taut pull of denim along his thigh as he swung one booted foot back and forth.

"I outgrew the fairy tales," he replied quietly, as if that would explain everything.

Consuelo frowned. "Then I feel sorry for you. What else do you have to look forward to, besides making a lot of money?"

He met her glance. "Money isn't all bad, Connie. It helped me renovate Lupe's home. It helps me give to the church and it keeps some of the wives in Sandera happy because their husbands are bringing home paychecks."

Consuelo thought about what she'd done to the bulldozer. "Can't you at least wait until after the festival? People have already made plans for it."

"Time is money, Connie, and shame on you for trying to use nasty tactics to make me change my mind. Speaking of which, did you happen to see who sabotaged my bulldozer?"

Although her heart pounded with guilt, she turned her most innocent expression on him. "Why, no. Did something happen?"

He smiled and glanced at her mouth. "Nothing that can't be repaired."

"Well, that's good, Ramón. I'm glad you have enough money to fix anything you want. Anything but what's most important. But then I suppose you've lost sight of that." She stood up, anger evident in the set of her chin.

"We seem to differ on what's important," he countered. "Just because I've taken the realistic stance to do what I believe, it doesn't make me any different from you."

They were both angry. It was Ramón who decided to push the envelope.

"Who knows, maybe after all this is over, we can sit down somewhere and talk about something other than the shrine."

"In your dreams." She felt a tiny shiver run through her body as she recalled the erotic dreams she'd been having about him. "I'll leave you to your work; after all, time is money," she spat out.

"In your case, I might be tempted to play hooky." His eyes searched hers for a reaction.

"Sorry, my time is up," she said, glancing at her watch. "I have another engagement. I'll just leave these here." She dropped several legal-sized sheets on his desk. "It's a copy. Something for you to think about." She walked to the door.

"Where are you running to? I thought changing my mind was a priority."

She turned and gave him a Mona Lisa smile. "Good-bye, Ramón. Do look over the petition. I believe Rafael's and Josie's names are on there. Bye." She smiled and waved.

That evening, during one of her busiest nights at the restaurant, a messenger approached and handed her a brown envelope. Curious, she made the mistake of opening it in front of the diners, most of whom were on the Women's Shrine Festival Committee. Lidia sat at a nearby table with her husband, Juan. Berta and her husband had joined them for the evening.

As Consuelo turned the envelope sideways to open the flap, tiny shredded pieces of paper fluttered to the floor, some of which were from the unmistakable blue legal cover sheet she'd stapled to the petition.

She glanced up in time to see Lidia's face take on a jaundiced color as she stared at the confetti. And as the implication of what it meant hit her, she turned grief-stricken eyes toward Consuelo.

His message was crystal clear. *Go to hell,* it told her.

By the time Enrique came over and vacuumed the mess, Consuelo was fuming. She continued to fume for the rest of the night. *¡Bastardo!* How dare he embarrass her like that.

That night, after she closed the restaurant, she sat at the dining room table with an untouched glass of iced tea in front of her. She tapped one long polished nail against the side of the glass and stared blankly at the Diego Rivera print on the wall.

"You're doing that infernal tapping again," Luna muttered.

Consuelo flinched. "And you're sneaking up on me again. I wish you'd give me some warning when you're coming into a room. One would think those boots would make a lot more noise."

"I saw the confetti. A love letter?"

"Hardly. It was the petition I left with Ramón today. Sometimes I wish . . ."

"Yes?"

"That he wasn't such a pain in the ass."

Luna laughed, then sobered as she noted the strained set of her sister's mouth.

"So what are you going to do about it?"

"I'm not sure. Any suggestions?"

Luna gave her a lopsided smile. "I take it the confetti was his counteraction to our little visit to the bulldozer the other night."

"Don't remind me."

Luna picked up Consuelo's iced tea and took a sip. "You just have to figure out another strategy."

"Easy for you to say, you're bloodthirsty."

Luna took another sip and set the glass down. "What would get him to change his mind, do you know?"

"Hard to say. I used to think I knew him, but he's changed. He's heartless and cynical, and he's probably got a vendetta against me."

Luna shrugged. "I don't think he'd purposely hurt you. He's come back to town to show you that he made something of his life, and having done so, he can't back down now. Men have this weird, disgusting macho insecurity they try to hide."

"When did you learn so much about men?" Consuelo asked.

"I've been reading relationship books."

They exchanged smiles.

"I guess I'll go ahead and try to get an injunction," Consuelo said. "All I need to do is slow him down until after the festival."

"Good luck." Luna yawned.

Consuelo waited until Luna had left the room before she allowed herself to feel the bleakness of her situation. *Of their situation.* Why did it have to be Ramón who'd bought the property?

She drooped like an unwatered flower as a heaviness settled over her heart, threatening to pull her under. She didn't want to fight him, and she didn't want the depressing job of feeling responsible for these people.

She was caught in the middle and, like it or not, she'd come too far to give up now.

A week later, the town was twittering over the latest news. Everyone had it on good authority that Consuelo had been spotted at the Oyster Bar and Grill with none other than Judge Reyes. Word had it that any day now, he planned to issue an injunction. The men rallied for Ramón while all the women marched around like little soldiers preparing for war.

Soon after, Ramón and Raul were seen at the same restaurant, dining with two Barbie lookalikes. No one made any comment except to say that the Oyster Bar and Grill had gotten very popular all of a sudden.

Eight

When everyone heard that Judge Reyes had issued an injunction, the air was charged with excitement. Consuelo had pulled it off again.

After the bulldozer and injunction incidents, a new respect rose for Consuelo. Some of the women began to wear red in her honor and the men, while not entirely sympathetic, took up their own form of support. They made wagers as to who would end up the victor. So far, Consuelo and Ramón were running neck and neck. At least that's what the men told their wives in order to keep peace at home.

Then something came to light that upped the ante. News traveled via the grapevine chatter that Consuelo and Ramón had shared a heated kiss beneath the sacred tree. And if they'd done that, what else had they shared?

The possibilities fueled their imaginations and heightened expectations.

Consuelo began to feel as though she was trapped in some *telenovela* that was going nowhere, although, to her delight, her restaurant business picked up. After all, she was worthy news. Her notoriety had other repercussions as well.

Suitors began to come out of the woodwork—in all sizes, shapes, and occupations. Some of them were handsome, too.

In any case, Consuelo was now in great demand. She was beautiful, courageous, and loyal—traits that made her a perfect baby-maker. The fact that she was in her thirties only made it more interesting; they knew that sooner or later, her biological clock would start ticking. And wasn't it nice that she loved children and strays? If she was a little too independent and opinionated, well, what did it matter? One couldn't have everything.

"I'm beginning to hate this," she told Luna one afternoon as she paced back and forth in her bedroom. "Everyone is so happy about the injunction, but what they don't know is that it's only for two weeks. The festival is three and a half weeks away. I don't have the heart to tell them."

"Why did the judge only grant you two weeks?"

Consuelo stopped pacing. "Maybe because Ramón got to him after I did. The snake had the audacity to invite the judge to dinner at *my* restaurant. I even saw them clinking glasses. I'm surprised he's not over here flaunting his treachery in my face."

"Why not talk to him again?"

"Never!"

"Offer him a compromise."

Consuelo stared at her sister as though she'd taken leave of her senses. "There can be no compromise, Luna. Either the tree stays or it goes. We want it to stay."

"You could offer to buy the property from him.

He wouldn't lose his money, everyone would have the tree, and the festival would go on as planned."

Consuelo looked skeptical. "It's a good idea, but I'm not sure he'll go for it."

Luna shrugged. "It's worth a try, isn't it?"

Consuelo's good mood returned. "Definitely worth a try," she said, glancing at her watch. "I'll go see him now."

Ramón's door was locked. Crestfallen, Consuelo wondered where he'd gone. Maybe he'd taken a late lunch somewhere. Maybe he was with Esperanza or the Barbie look-alike. The thought made her frown.

She was searching in her purse for a pen and something to write on when he pulled up and got out of his car.

"I was just getting ready to leave you a note," she said a little breathlessly.

He looked genuinely surprised to see her. "I had some business to go over with Raul." He unlocked the door and waited for her to enter.

"I can't stay long," she said. "I have another appointment."

"Really? Where? I'm intrigued." He propped his arm on top of the filing cabinet.

She shrugged a delicate shoulder. "I doubt it would be of any interest to you."

"How do you know? Try me."

"It's personal." She smiled and changed the subject. "But I have something that might be of interest."

His eyes were appraising as they took in her white sundress, and he noted she looked much shorter today. She came up to just below his chin. His gaze dropped to the white sandals, and he smiled.

"Go ahead. I'm all ears."

Finding herself suddenly nervous, Consuelo cleared her throat. Wondering how best to broach the subject, she decided on a straightforward approach. "Would you consider selling the land?"

"Not really."

"You want a piece of property where you can build your mall. We want the tree to live, so what if we could raise the money?"

"I've already lined up contracts and appointments. I'm on a timeline here."

She stared silently out the window. It had started to drizzle, and she watched the rain bead its way down the glass. He would never change his mind. She knew that now, and she wanted to take her fist and hit it against the pane from sheer frustration.

Bracing her shoulders, she turned to him. "Then I guess we're at a stalemate."

Having nothing else to say, she simply walked away.

Ramón watched her cross the street and enter her restaurant. She'd been calm. Too calm, and he wondered what she was thinking.

He sighed in exasperation. He could see how she would think that he'd bought the property for personal reasons, and that it might smack of the settling of scores. But he hadn't thought of it that way. Or had he? He'd loved her, had shared a lot with her, and he'd wanted to believe that she could never wound him like she had. Still, he could never hurt her, no matter what.

He looked out the window and saw her come back out, this time with a large grocery sack in her arms. He tapped his pen absently on the desk as he watched her climb into her car.

He knew where she was going. However, he was surprised to see she still wore the white sundress and sandals. He'd expected her to change into jeans.

By the time her Riviera rounded the corner, he'd picked up his car keys and was on his way out the door.

Consuelo pitched the milk cartons and Coke cans into the brown sack and began gathering the tiny figures she'd purchased at a toy store. She'd wanted something smaller to practice with today and had tucked the toy figures in various locations—on the tree, on the log, and hanging from branches.

She stretched her arms high above her head. It had been a stressful day, and she'd needed something else on which to concentrate her energies. Practicing with that whip certainly took the edge off her anger.

The sky was overcast, and in the distance she heard a rumble. She quickly threw the bag and whip in the trunk of her car and closed it, then turned and glanced wistfully toward the river. She hadn't been able to go for a swim the last couple of times she'd been here, and she was drawn to do so now. Why not? she thought. Juana and Luna were taking care of things at the restaurant and it was her cousin Maria's turn to help with the cooking. And it had been so long since she'd felt wild and carefree.

The water, so inviting, had Consuelo slipping off her sandals and stripping down to her white cotton slip in record time. She laid the clothes in a neat pile on the ground nearby and, as she stepped into the cool river, the thin straps of her slip were already sliding off her shoulders.

She waded out a few feet and stopped. The water came to just below her chest, deep enough for the moment, and fun to play in. The water was so clear she could see her toes. She squatted and disappeared beneath the water, only to come back up with her hair dripping wet. She wished she could swim in the nude, but didn't feel comfortable doing that here. Again, she heard thunder. *Stay away . . . just a little longer.*

Forgetting everything but how good she felt, Consuelo floated on her back. She enjoyed the cool tranquility, aware of how different the sky looked from this angle. Entranced, she studied the roiling clouds, so dark and forbidding.

Closing her eyes, she drifted for a moment, intent on enjoying whatever time she had left. She heard thunder again, only this time it sounded much closer.

* * *

Ramón halted Diablo under the same tree as before. He called himself all kinds of fool for coming here and intruding on her privacy. He watched her as she floated on her back, the peaks of her breasts barely peeking above the water.

The wind picked up, rippling the meadow grass. Diablo pranced nervously. "Easy, boy."

A moment later, he spurred Diablo to the water's edge. The stallion whinnied, but Consuelo didn't seem to hear; she was busy humming a song off-key.

Ramón felt like a voyeur and wondered how to make his presence known. He hesitated calling out to her for fear of frightening her.

He watched her stand and noticed the water came to just below her breasts. Her eyes were closed and she raised her arms to lift the wet hair from her neck. He swallowed uncomfortably as she stretched, her movements slow, lazy, and damned seductive.

She brought her arms down slowly and began to submerge herself under the water again.

"Beautiful day, isn't it?"

She came up sputtering, wiping water from her eyes, and then she turned to face him, shock in her eyes.

"Ramón, what are you doing here?"

He leaned back in his saddle. "I might ask you the same thing."

"I *was* enjoying my day, and you're not supposed to be here."

His gaze shifted lazily toward her clothes lying on the ground before returning to her. "I'm not the one who's trespassing." He got off the horse but stayed where he was.

Consuelo eyed him suspiciously. "I have permission to be here."

"Last time I checked, this is my land."

"Raul owns it, too."

"Not this part. Before Dad died, he let us choose which third of the ranch we wanted. And you're standing on my third."

"Naturally." She frowned. "You've made your point. I'll be gone in a minute." A second later, her eyes widened as he took two steps toward her. "Wait a minute, what are you doing?"

"You look like you're having so much fun, I thought maybe I'd join you," he said, meaning only to tease her.

She held up a warning hand. "Stay right there. I'd like to get out."

"All right."

"If you'll turn around, I'll be on my way."

When he made no move to comply, her eyes narrowed dangerously. "You *are* going to be a gentlemen about this and turn your back, aren't you?"

His eyes took on a stubborn gleam. "No."

"No?"

Ramón crossed his arms and shook his head. He knew he should be ashamed of himself for teasing her. He was about to tell her he'd give her some privacy, but before he could do so, Consuelo was climbing up on the bank, water dripping from her hair and body. She had some flimsy thing on that clung to her body like a second skin and rode up her thighs. Its thin straps had slipped off her shoulders and her nipples strained against the fabric. He felt his pulse quicken.

His gaze licked her body hungrily as tiny droplets of water beaded on her long, spiky lashes and shoulders. He didn't realize what he was doing until she spoke up.

"Do close your mouth, Ramón, it's in danger of catching flies. And just because I've gained a few pounds doesn't mean I'm a prude."

He rallied enough to smile. "Well, wherever they are, they're lucky, and I envy them their attachment."

"Now you're making fun of me," she said, squeezing water from her hair and slip. She was standing beside her clothes, but made no move to put them on.

Ramón felt a strong urge to kiss her eyes, her mouth, her body, and he could tell by the darkening of her eyes that she felt the palpable chemistry between them.

He reached her in two strides. His index finger touched her cheek gently before continuing a lazy path to play with one of her straps.

"I would never make fun of you." His voice was low and husky. "You look cold," he said, gazing downward.

"I . . . I am," she said, shivering, but whether from the wet clothing or his nearness, she couldn't say.

"Maybe we should get you out of those wet clothes."

Not waiting for a reply, he lowered his mouth to hers. Consuelo closed her eyes and clutched his shoulders, pressing closer to his warmth, his hardness. His lips moved against hers with urgency, demanding, taking. His mouth left hers, trailing kisses down her neck, lower still until he reached one hardened bud. She could feel the heat of his mouth on her nipple through her wet slip.

His long fingers seared a path along her quivering skin and slid beneath the tiny straps, easing them down over her soft shoulders, lower still until he could relish the swelling fullness of her breast. As his tongue circled a hardened pink-tipped nipple, a small moan escaped her throat.

"Oh, Ramón."

"What, baby?" he whispered against her skin.

She felt so weak she could hardly stand, but she wanted him to know how she felt. "I'm so glad you met me here. I never stopped caring about you."

His muscles went taut and something in his eyes flickered. For anyone else, those would've been happy words; however, for Ramón they were like a douse of cold water in his face. The memory of how he'd waited for her here on this spot seven years ago and she'd never shown up still rankled. His wound was still too raw, and he pulled away. How could he want her this bad after she'd made a fool of him? For a moment the old pain came back to bite him and he shuddered.

"Ramón, what's wrong?" she asked, missing his nearness.

"If you cared about me, you had an odd way of showing it," he replied without emotion.

She stared at him, wishing for a moment she'd kept quiet. But now that everything was out in the open, she wanted him to know the truth. "I wanted to marry you!" She lifted her straps to hide her nakedness.

"But you went straight to another man's arms."

"It wasn't like that, and I had no other choice."

"We all have choices. You made yours."

"I need to tell you what happened. Get angry at me if you want, but give me a chance to explain."

"I have to go."

"Ramón, please stay." She hated begging. She was shaking, not from being cold, but from his refusal to listen to her.

He was walking away.

Panic gripped her. She knew if he walked away from her now, something important would slip away and she'd never get it back. She had to make him listen.

"Stop, Ramón. I mean it." A pulse throbbed angrily in her neck and she stooped down and grabbed the closest thing to her.

The crack of the whip shattered the silence.

Ramón came to a halt and flinched, grabbing his shoulder.

Consuelo knew she'd drawn blood. Oh, God, she'd gone too far. And she had hurt him again, only this time it was physically. She watched him turn to face her, his features expressing a mixture of anger, surprise, and pain.

Her voice quivered in anger and something else. Remorse. "You never even tried to fight for me. You abandoned me. And I had no choice but

to go through with it," she cried. He'd been everything to her, and she'd been so hurt that he could
leave her so easily without giving her a chance to
explain.

He walked toward her with a catlike gait, ignoring the blood on his arm and the tears in her
eyes. When he reached her something shifted in
his eyes as they raked over her.

"What do you want to hear? That you hurt me?
But you knew that already. I suppose you want to
hear something that will assuage your guilt?" He
looked away and when he glanced back at her, his
features were uncompromising.

"No, Connie," he said softly. "The time for talk
is over." He reached out and pulled her to him,
and his mouth took possession of hers again, this
time with a savage need.

She fought to steady her senses but his mouth,
warm and rough against hers, pulled her back
into the memories—to the past and how it had
been between them. Her arms wound themselves
around his neck again, just as they'd done a thousand times before.

His kiss was long and hungry as his tongue invaded her mouth, searching for her tongue. A light
drizzle had begun to fall and he pulled away long
enough to pick her up in his arms and carry her to
a spot beneath a tree, where he set her down.

"I'm going to make love to you. But first we
need to get rid of this," he said, ripping her slip
from her body and letting it drop to the ground.

He shed his clothes and threw them on the
ground until they were standing a heartbeat away

from each other. He coaxed her to lie on the ground, then reached out and touched her cheek tenderly. This time his mouth moved over her lips slowly, gently.

Beads of rain clung to branches and the air was filled with the scent of trees and damp earth.

His mouth and hands devoured her, touching her everywhere. His hand slid down her body to her thighs, his touch exploring, demanding her surrender. She clutched him, wanting him inside her.

He paused long enough to reach for the wallet in his trousers and take out one of the foil packets.

A moment later, his shaft found her, then slowly slid home. She moaned against his mouth as he stretched and filled her, then moved within her. His heart beat a rhythm against her own. Hot and wet, they lost themselves in each other.

Afterward, she didn't know how long they lay there. A light drizzle continued to fall, but the threat of a storm had passed. Every now and then she heard thunder, but it was so far away that it didn't matter. She glanced at Ramón and saw he was watching her. He stood up and leaned over her.

"Give me your hand," he ordered. When she complied, he helped her up, then carried her into the water and set her down, pressing himself against her.

"I want you again," he said thickly. His hands encircled her waist and lifted her until she could feel his erection between her thighs. As she wrapped her legs around him, he lifted her slightly and his hands moved to her bottom, then he eased her down and sank himself inside her.

Water swirled and lapped around them. The drizzle came down harder now, streaming down her cheeks and mingling with the tears running down her face. She clung to him as if she never wanted to let him go.

He looked deeply into her eyes. "I want you more than I ever thought possible. Love me," he whispered into her mouth, "for as long as it lasts."

Her heart cried out, eager to meet each thrust, wanting to tell him she loved him.

"Yes," she cried.

Later, when he walked her to her car, he kissed her lightly. She dreaded for the afternoon to end, but she didn't fool herself into believing he would forgive her so easily.

"I'll see you later," he said.

But she couldn't leave without talking it through. She had to finish this. "I never meant to hurt you . . . I never stopped loving you."

His glance moved over her, but no longer with desire. This time there was a flash of anger in his eyes.

"Since I feel obligated to answer, I can only say that you had an odd way of showing it."

"Believe me, if I could go back and change things, I would."

He frowned. "Was it worth throwing half our lives away? Did you lie awake at night wondering how it could have been with us? Did you make yourself sick wondering if I lay with another woman? I hope so. It should have been *our* time. We could've had children. No one could have loved you more than I."

His words tore at her heart. "Ramón, I . . ." She could barely get the words past the lump in her throat. "My family needed me."

"Dammit! *I* needed you."

"I'm sorry." Simple words were often the most difficult.

"Sorry doesn't make it feel any better." With an air of resignation, he shrugged. "It doesn't really matter anymore, because I can never trust you again," he said grimly.

His words hung in the air before the wind carried them away, leaving behind an overwhelming sense of loss, of loneliness.

He hurried to his horse.

"Ramón, forgive me," she whispered.

He didn't bother to look back. She stood there under a sky of dying violet and watched her last dash of hope disappear. Whatever she'd felt seven years ago couldn't compare to the sense of utter desolation she felt at this moment.

She'd lost him twice.

Nine

The town knew something was wrong. They couldn't quite put their finger on what it was, but they knew. For one thing, both Consuelo and Ramón kept pretty much to themselves. For another, Consuelo had lost much of her sparkle and she didn't come out and greet her customers as often as she'd done in the past. It was a sad situation for everyone concerned.

Then Consuelo informed the Women's Shrine Festival Committee that the temporary injunction had run its course. Ramón could resume work on his land. She was sorry, but there was nothing else she could do.

They thanked her and told her she'd done everything she could, and then they waited for a miracle to occur. After all, everyone knew that God answered prayers. Maybe not always in the way one expected, but He answered them nevertheless.

However, it wouldn't hurt to try something else, just in case God didn't intervene in time. It was too late for council meetings, useless court interventions, or last-minute begging. So far, their pleas had fallen on deaf ears. With the festival a week and a half away, they decided to give Fate a push.

The left side of the property had already been leveled and, to everyone's horror, the bulldozer had reached the tree. Then, to their relief, Fred, the bulldozer man (as everyone referred to him now), began leveling the right side. Another reprieve, but for how long? And did this mean that Ramón was beginning to change his mind? Or was he merely playing with their emotions?

Impatient, Lidia Sanchez called a secret meeting at her home. Only certain members were invited to attend: her twin, Loretta, Lena Morales, Esperanza, and, surprisingly, Luna, but only because Esperanza had sung her praises. Luna was a rebel; she wouldn't take guff off of anyone, and besides, she'd fought for causes on campus. No one thought to ask if she'd been successful. Berta had sadly declined the invitation; she'd been a victim of a botched hair-dye experiment and was rushing out to buy toner, but promised to meet with them later.

With the overwhelming desperation of the hopeless, they exhausted all ideas but one. It would certainly bring repercussions, but they had to give it one last try.

By the time they concluded their meeting and had sworn each other to secrecy, their emotions, while not charged with excitement, were at least filled with the sense of assurance that one way or another, there would be closure of some sort.

As they filed out of Lidia's home, she reminded them not to forget their motto: *Be Fearless!*

Outside, they noticed that the peaceful blue sky had been replaced by dark, angry clouds.

Consuelo had three days of uneasy peace. Work on Ramón's property had stalled due to rain. Not heavy, but steady. And during those three days, she'd not seen or heard from him.

Once, he had loved her; but now, for all she knew, as soon as his obligation with the construction of his mall was complete, he would leave Sandera.

As long as it lasts, he'd said, and she had no illusions as to what that meant. It sounded pretty temporary to her. Of course, that wasn't even an option anymore. He'd made it pretty clear what he thought of her now.

Forcing a polite smile, Consuelo ushered an elderly couple to a table and handed each a menu. Embarrassingly, her stomach rumbled as she walked away, and with good reason. She hadn't eaten all day.

When she entered the kitchen, Sophia had just finished her dinner. "You ready to eat?"

Consuelo shook her head. "Maybe later."

"The rain is keeping people away tonight," Sophia told her.

"Most likely. Why don't you go on home. I'm closing early."

Later in her bedroom, she remembered she still hadn't eaten and her stomach rumbled again. She went to her small kitchen and poured herself a glass of milk.

Luna had gone home for a couple of days, and Consuelo found that she missed her. At least Luna had been right about one thing, she thought, as she flicked off the light and slipped into bed. The dreams had stopped. Now when she slept, she was usually exhausted.

In an effort not to think about him, she had kept as busy as she could. All of a sudden, when she wasn't working in the restaurant, she fell into a cleaning frenzy—floors, furniture and walls. She even went through several boxes she had stashed in the attic, pitched what she no longer needed, and thought long and hard about what she kept. Those who knew her well would have said she was trying to clean up her life. One of the boxes contained mementos—photos, concert tickets—of events she'd shared with Ramón. She couldn't bear to go through them, so she returned the box to the attic.

Now as she lay in bed, she listened to thousands of tiny fingers of rain tapping against her bedroom window. Soon, the rain lulled her into a restless sleep.

Some time later, a noise woke her and Consuelo opened her eyes. For a moment, she lay still, waiting; then she heard it again—a pinging sound.

Something was hitting against one of her French doors, and she rose cautiously to see what it was. The rain had nearly stopped, but she could still make out a light drizzle as she peered through the lace curtains of one of the doors. She looked down at the water-slick street and, beneath the soft lamplight, she saw someone standing under her balcony, staring up at her window.

Surprise lit her features as she recognized Ramón. He was about to throw another pebble up when she opened the door.

"What are you doing?"

"I'd like to talk to you."

"At midnight?"

"Will you open up for me?"

She noted that he seemed visibly upset. "Can you come around back to the kitchen?"

He nodded and disappeared.

She hurried down the stairs and hit the dimmer light switch on the kitchen wall just before she unlocked the door to let him in.

"I apologize if I woke you. I thought since you closed at ten, that you usually went to bed around now."

"I do, but I closed early tonight." She motioned for him to have a seat at the kitchen table. "Would you like coffee or tea or a beer?"

"I don't need any more coffee. A beer will be fine."

She padded over to the fridge, took out a beer, and handed it to him, then sat down across from him.

"Thanks." He pulled back the tab and took a swig.

She waited for him to speak. He glanced around the room until finally, he leaned back and sighed. "After the way I left you at the river, I can understand if you don't want to speak to me again, but I need to talk to you about something."

"All right," she replied warily, wondering what could make him worried enough to come by at this hour.

"I've been walking around and thinking. On my way back, I decided on the spur of the moment to see you. I apologize for awakening you," he repeated.

"I'm listening."

He could see she still looked half asleep and he was tempted to reach out and cup her cheek, to tell her he was sorry, that he wished things could have happened differently at the river and that everything could be all right between them. But things weren't right, and he couldn't pretend otherwise. Still, he could at least put her mind and his at ease about one thing.

His fingers tightened around the beer can. "I owe you an apology. I overreacted the other day and no matter how upset I've been over the past, it's my problem and I'll have to learn to deal with it."

She remained silent, not really knowing what to say. But he didn't seem to expect an answer. He ran his fingers through his already disheveled hair.

Her heart was breaking and all she could think about was how terribly tempted she was to run her fingers through the silky texture of his long hair. And as hard as she tried to forget the day at the river, she couldn't. It *had* happened. It was no use now to explain to him why she'd married Tomas. It wouldn't help erase his pain any more than it would hers. Regret. Missed opportunities. What did it all matter now? There was too much water under the bridges that she'd burned.

He cleared his throat. "What happened between us the other day shouldn't have happened, but it did and we just have to move on. But I want to put your mind at ease. I don't plan on having it happen again, so you don't have to worry that I'll make any demands on you." He set the beer can on the table.

She nodded, suddenly uncomfortable. She could have told him not to worry, that she had no intention of making any demands on him. She just didn't have the energy, nor did she feel like talking about it right now, so she simply said, "As you wish."

She must've appeared uninterested and unemotional, because his features turned stormy and he looked away.

"I'd better let you get some sleep," he said. "It's pretty late; someone's liable to see me leaving here."

Was he worrying about her reputation or his, she wondered. She stood up and walked him to the door.

She wanted to weep, wanted to yell, anything to make her angry enough to forget him. Instead, she closed the door and rested her forehead on its cool surface. He hadn't even wanted to know how she felt about him, or maybe he'd figured emotions had too high a price. Tears rolled down her cheeks but she didn't bother to wipe them away.

Each time she saw him, her pain got a little

worse. And tomorrow would be no different. She would see him again.

She had promised to attend her goddaughter, Rafaella's, birthday party.

The first thing she saw was Ramón's truck parked in the driveway of Rafael and Josie's home. Rafael had built the red, slate-roofed adobe home for Jose and their children on his part of the ranch. Oak trees provided shade, and the grass, a healthy green, looked stark against the eggshell-colored adobe.

Fuchsia-colored azaleas lined the walk, and Consuelo admired them as she climbed three steps to the porch and rang the doorbell. When Josie answered the door, she grinned.

"Hi, come on in. Glad you could make it," Josie said, giving her a hug.

Consuelo heard a shriek behind her and turned to see Rafaella wobbling toward her.

"She's learned to walk," Josie bragged proudly.

Excitement spread across Rafaella's tiny features as Consuelo scooped her up and planted a kiss on her cheek.

"How's my favorite girl?" Consuelo asked laughingly, enjoying her baby smell and her chubby hands.

"Da," Rafaella cried as she pointed to the gift in Consuelo's hand.

Josie grinned. "She calls everyone *da*. Rafael gets a big kick out of it."

Consuelo grinned and handed her the gift.

Rafaella answered by shaking the gift, then circling her chubby arms around Consuelo's neck and hugging her.

"She doesn't care a lick about the gifts, but she loves those bows."

Consuelo was glad she'd bought the brightest wrapping paper and bow. "Where is everyone?" she asked.

"The guys are out back cooking steaks. What would you like to drink?"

Consuelo thought a moment. "A cola." Rafaella wiggled to be released, and Consuelo set her down and watched as she wobbled over to her mother, excitedly showing her the bright red bow on the gift.

"I'm surprised she's not tearing it open just so she can play with the wrapping paper," Consuelo said.

Josie eyed her daughter. "Me too. I went ahead and fed her since I know she's going to wear herself out soon and get sleepy."

Consuelo nodded in understanding. "I just love that child. She's so beautiful." Consuelo meant every word.

"She's crazy about you and you know it," Josie said, handing her a Coke. "Come on, let's go see everyone."

Consuelo couldn't delay it any longer. She'd have to face him sooner or later. It might as well be now. She dropped her purse on the couch and headed outside.

As soon as they stepped out on the patio, all conversation stopped. The only sound was the music on the CD player. All three brothers stared at Consuelo.

"Hi there, is this a private party or can anyone join?" She smiled.

Rafael immediately walked over and embraced her. "I'm glad you could make it. Did Luna come with you?"

"No. She went home for the weekend and I haven't spoken to her. Maybe she'll come by later." Raul hugged her next. When it came time to say hello to Ramón, she merely nodded.

He was standing in front of the barbeque pit turning a steak and he waved. Diego and Elena Castillo also came forward, along with Ben Solis, who grabbed her. "Hey, Connie, great to see you!"

"Hi, everyone! Where's Miguel?"

A short distance away, Miguel, playing with two other friends, heard his name and came running over.

"Hola, sweetheart."

Miguel smiled and hugged her.

She bent down and whispered, "There's a gift for you inside my purse. I couldn't bring a gift to my goddaughter without giving one to my favorite guy, now, could I?"

He smiled. "But my birthday isn't until next month. I'll be nine," he said proudly.

"Well, I'll just have to bring another one then, won't I?"

"Thanks. Is it okay if I open mine up after my sister opens hers?"

"Of course it's okay." Consuelo hugged him again. She'd loved this child from the first mo-

ment she'd seen him just after Josie had been
brought to the hospital after the mugging.

Consuelo looked up in time to see Rafaella at-
tempt to run to her dad without much success.
He met her halfway and picked her up in his
arms, then danced her around the patio.

"Da," she said and shook the brightly colored
gift, almost hitting him in the face. He dodged it
and everyone laughed.

True to her word, Josie brought the presents
outside and proceeded to let Rafaella open them.
Eventually Josie had to help her open the gifts.
Rafaella seemed content with just playing with the
wrapping paper.

"She's so excited because everyone is here, but
I bet it won't be long before she's asleep."

"The food's done," Ramón shouted, and then
received answering yells and whoops of hungry
stomachs.

While Rafaella played with a Barbie, everyone
gathered around the picnic table to eat. To Consuelo's surprise, Ramón sat next to her, and she
felt awkward when their shoulders touched as he
leaned over to reach for a flour tortilla.

She wondered how she was going to get
through the meal but she did, and afterward
when a salsa started to play in the background,
Rafaella came over and held out her hands. Consuelo picked her up and twirled her around.
Rafaella held on and laughed, sputtering unintel-
ligible words.

Ramón felt his throat tighten as he watched
Consuelo's shapely body move to the music. Right

now, with her peasant off-shoulder blouse and the thick mane of hair falling nearly to her waist, she looked like a tawny-skinned gypsy. She'd always been a good dancer. She'd also been such a natural with kids. That was one of the things he'd loved about her, and he wondered why she hadn't had children. His next thought was that he wished she'd had his, but just as quickly he tamped the thought down. He'd promised himself he wouldn't think of the past.

Rafaella wiggled out of Consuelo's arms and returned to playing with one of her toys.

"Is there anything I can do to help?" Consuelo asked Josie.

"No, everything's under control."

A *cumbia* started playing, and Raul grabbed Consuelo around the waist. "Let's dance."

Consuelo hesitated for a moment, then smiled. "After the other day when you almost caused me to hurt poor Ramón here, I'm not sure I should dance with you. You're dangerous."

He laughed. "We'll try it again and this time, I won't twirl you. I'll just keep you in my arms. My dear brother wouldn't know what to do with you if you landed on his lap."

Ramón let the remark pass, but he frowned dangerously as he watched them dance. He almost came close to calling his brother out; however, he refrained from doing so. Raul had known about him and Consuelo. Hell, the whole town had known how he'd felt about her. That's why he'd left town. He wouldn't have been able to get through the stares or people feeling sorry for him. Just the same, he found he wanted to break Raul's arms.

Consuelo was laughing at something Raul had said when someone tapped him on the shoulder. It was Ramón.

"Can I cut in or is this a private showing?"

Raul smiled. "For once, *hermano*, you're showing good judgment. Be my guest."

Ramón again ignored the barb as he took Consuelo into his arms. A tango began to play—music as old as time with a rhythm that made one's pulse beat faster. Ramón's arm held her close as he took her through the most passionate of moves, urging her to move with him.

Their eyes locked, and for a moment there was no one else but them—no past, no future, only the present.

He had always enjoyed dancing with her, but most of all, he had loved the mutual passion that had burned like the heat of summer. Now, as he gazed into her eyes, he noticed hers were wary.

He tightened his hold on her waist and pulled her closer, drawing her into the rhythm of the music. As their eyes met again, he was almost ready to believe that anything was possible.

The shrill ring of a phone rent the air and they both came back to earth. It took Ramón a moment to realize that it was his cell phone that was ringing, and reluctantly he reached into his jeans pocket to answer it. When he hung up and looked at her, all traces of desire were gone and he was frowning.

He spoke to Rafael and Josie. "I have to go." He

turned to Consuelo. "It seems your little old ladies are on my land, demonstrating."

Consuelo's brows furrowed. "Demonstrating what?"

"The tree is being bulldozed today. Lidia Sanchez and her followers have surrounded the tree. I've got to get over there."

So enraptured by the gleam in Ramón's eyes, Consuelo had forgotten all about the tree. She hadn't known that he planned to get rid of it today. Why hadn't he mentioned that last night?

Rafael's phone rang and when he hung up, he was already grabbing his keys. "Xavier can't seem to get the women away from the tree." He kissed Josie. "I'll be back just as soon as I can, honey." Then he bent down and kissed his daughter good-bye.

Ramón turned to Consuelo, his eyes accusing. "I think you'd better get on over there, too. Your sister's one of them."

She returned his stare with an angry one of her own. While he'd been here enjoying the afternoon and known she'd be here, too, he'd plotted to finish the job. Damn him!

Struggling to control her anger, she hugged Josie. "I'd better go, but I'm really sorry this is ruining your day and Rafaella's."

"Don't worry about her, she's had a wonderful day, and look at her, she's so tired her eyes are drooping. She would've forced herself to stay awake."

"Let's get together again soon," Consuelo called over her shoulder as she ran toward her car.

Josie waved good-bye. "Call me and good luck."

Consuelo started up her car and eased out onto the road. She knew why the women were retaliating, but what in the world had Luna been thinking? Why was she getting mixed up in all of this? And why hadn't Consuelo suspected something?

Of course, she knew the answer. She'd been going around moping, feeling sorry for herself when she should've been backing them. While she'd been dancing with Ramón, the women had been suffering, waiting for the ax to fall. She should've shown more support. Instead, Luna had taken her place. She felt her chest tighten. She'd failed them.

She floored the accelerator.

Consuelo pulled up in the restaurant's parking lot and slammed on her brakes. She climbed out of the car and ran across the street. She couldn't see the women because a crowd had gathered.

A deputy warned people to stand back or leave, but the crowd stood its ground.

By the time Consuelo was finally able to see the situation, she wanted to weep. A handful of women, led no doubt by Lidia Sanchez, had chained themselves to the tree and were now glaring at the ugly piece of machinery that stood like a warrior mere inches away, daring it to come any closer.

Ten

The crowd gathering to watch was growing. Two deputies were already on the scene, one directing traffic while the other kept warning people to stay back. Sheriff Rafael Santos looked more amused than angry.

A couple of people craned their necks and stepped around the deputy in order to get a better view. A minute later, Andy Perez, a reporter for the *Sandera Gazette,* ambled up. He was certain he'd come to see history in the making and he wanted to be sure to get plenty of pictures.

Consuelo approached Ramón, who eyed her with suspicion. Her nostrils flared. After yesterday's rain, the air smelled of freshly turned earth.

"Did you know they were going to do this?" he asked, gesturing to the women who stood stock-still, their shoulders squared.

Her chin lifted perceptibly. "No."

"How do I know you didn't plan it?"

"You'll just have to take my word for it. Why didn't you tell me you planned to get rid of the shrine today?" she asked in exasperation.

He shrugged. "You've known it would happen

sooner or later. I didn't feel like repeating myself."

"Yet you needled me about something *you* wanted to know about."

"That's different."

"Different? How so? As I recall, you had plenty of time to mention it."

She stared bleakly toward the women, remembering Ramón had mentioned Luna was involved. "Luna! What are you doing here?"

Luna looked out of place among the wrinkled, elderly women. That is, until Consuelo spotted Esperanza at the other end of the line.

"I'm fighting for our cause."

"Oh, Luna, there isn't any cause. Not anymore. You can't stop Ramón from building on his property."

Luna's eyes narrowed. "We can slow him down until we celebrate the festival."

Ramón was visibly angry now. "You women could've been hurt, you know that? Now I want you all to stop this crazy foolishness and hand over the key so that we can unchain you."

"We don't have it," Luna answered with a stubborn set to her mouth.

"What do you mean you don't have it? You must've had the key when you chained yourself to that tree," he said curtly.

For a moment, the only sound was a bird twittering at the top of the tree, letting everyone know he didn't appreciate his space being invaded.

Lidia finally spoke up. "Someone has it, but we're not talking."

Consuelo and Ramón stared at Luna suspiciously, ignoring the steady click of Andy Perez's camera.

Ramón wasn't in the mood for this farce. His eyes narrowed dangerously. "I ought to let you all stand there all day and see how you like it. What if Fred here had accidentally run over you?"

"Fred wouldn't dare," Lidia spouted. "He's already in deep, deep trouble with his wife." A limp wave of gray hair had fallen forward, almost obscuring part of her face.

Fred glanced nervously toward the crowd, searching for his wife. When he didn't see her, he relaxed slightly and shrugged.

"Who has the key?" Ramón asked again, getting angrier by the minute.

No one answered. Consuelo faced the women. "Ladies, there's nothing else we can do. For what it's worth, I'm sorry."

"This is all your fault for giving them hope. I want these women off my land."

Anger seeped out of Consuelo's pores and her hands shook. How dare he put them all through this hell?!

She took a deep breath. "Ladies, I know how you feel. I feel the same way, but it's no use. His mind is made up and nothing is going to change it. Go home. Please." Her voice broke and she fought to control it.

Her chin came up in an obstinate gesture as she faced Ramón. "Why couldn't you at least have let them celebrate the festival?"

"Not that old song again." He knew he was being unreasonable, but he couldn't help himself.

Years of pain and anger were resurfacing and he couldn't stop himself. He walked over to the women to check out the lock, just to make certain that it was locked and they weren't bluffing.

Consuelo heard the cold, metallic rattling of the chain.

"You heartless bastard! Get away from them!"

He turned slightly, although he kept his hands on the chain. *"I'm* heartless?" He gave a bitter laugh.

She stared him down. "At least I never hurt you intentionally, and if this is the way you turned out, then I thank my lucky stars I escaped."

"That makes two of us."

In two short strides, she reached him. Her heart was still pounding and her temples throbbed from anger. It happened so fast, she didn't have time to stop herself. She drew her hand back and slapped him.

Shocked gasps rose from the crowd. They couldn't believe their eyes. Meanwhile, Andy Perez's camera kept clicking away.

"You made your point," he said quietly.

Shocked that she could do such a thing, she cried out, "See what you've made me do?" The tears in her eyes were on the verge of escape until finally they broke through.

"What *I* made you do?"

"You've upset everyone, including me," she cried. "If you wanted to hurt me, then you've succeeded. You were my best friend once, my life, and now . . ." She swallowed painfully. "I wish you'd never come back."

Her words fell like the stroke of an ax. Shocked murmurs passed through the crowd, although no one could hear what she said next.

"You've won," she whispered with biting finality. She could barely make out Rafael through her tears as she shot past him.

Her words wrapped themselves like cold tentacles around Ramón's heart, and he felt the fight go out of him. He was disgusted with himself for hurting her, for hurting all of them. Why hadn't he just kept his mouth shut? Quietly, he walked over to Fred, who sat patiently on the bulldozer.

"We might as well quit for the day."

Fred nodded and jumped down from the machine. "You want me to come back tomorrow?"

He stared at Consuelo's back as she ran across the street. "I'll call and let you know." To the women, he said, "Go on home, folks. I think everyone's had enough excitement for one day."

From a short distance away, Rafael studied his brother. He'd taken in the situation, known it had been brewing for a while and decided not to interfere. Those two would have to work out their own problems. He walked away, shaking his head.

Now that Consuelo had left, and realizing there would be nothing else to see, the crowd began to disperse, seemingly tired of the whole thing.

Ramón walked away, not bothering to glance at the women.

Lidia's voice was subdued as she stared at Berta, who stood a few feet away. "Berta, could you please unlock this thing? The bark is beginning to dig into my back. Besides, I think we've done enough damage for one day."

After Berta had freed them, Esperanza faced Luna. "I feel just terrible," she wailed. "Please tell your sister we're sorry."

Luna nodded and swallowed, remorse pulling at her heart at seeing how hurt her sister had been. "I will. That is, if she's still speaking to me."

Saddened at how things had turned out this day, they each separated and walked off in different directions.

The following morning found Luna standing in Consuelo's bedroom, holding out a steaming cup of coffee as a peace offering. "I hope you're still speaking to me, *hermana.*"

Consuelo accepted the coffee gratefully. "I'm not angry at you."

Luna sat on the edge of the bed and faced Consuelo, who sat in a nearby overstuffed chair, staring down at the newspaper she held.

"I'm really sorry," she began again awkwardly. "So are the other women." Luna sighed deeply. "And I'm equally sorry you're hurting. Please talk to me," she pleaded.

Consuelo tore her gaze away from the caption below her photograph and glanced up. "It's all right, Luna. It isn't your fault. Everyone was doing what they felt they had to do."

Luna winced at how calm Consuelo was. It didn't seem natural somehow. "I see you and Ramón made the front page."

"Yes," Consuelo answered grimly as she stared down at the photograph of her slapping Ramón. She'd wept most of the night, and felt far from calm as she set the newspaper to one side. "I just wish it wouldn't hurt so much. I'll never be able to face Ramón again and I can barely breathe from the pain."

"I know, Sis." Luna patted Consuelo's shoulder. "I wish I could tell you that it's all going to turn out fine, that time will heal all wounds, but the truth of the matter is that I've never felt toward a man the way you've loved Ramón. All I can say is that I'm here for you."

Consuelo felt listless. "Thanks, that means a lot to me. The town had its heart set on having the festival. Now what will it do?"

Luna shrugged. "It isn't as if we couldn't have the festival. We'll just have to have it without the shrine."

"But the shrine is what makes the festival so special," Consuelo replied.

"The festival is only six days away. Whatever happens, I guess there's a reason for everything."

They sat for a moment in companionable silence until finally, Consuelo said, "I can't stay here. I have to leave."

"Leave?" Luna blinked in surprise. "What do you mean?"

"I need to get away for a few days."

Luna breathed a sigh of relief. "Thank goodness. I thought you meant for good." She frowned. "You're not going to let him scare you away, are you?"

"Not at all. I just have to go somewhere to think. Actually, I've been considering it for a while, and now would be as good a time as any."

Luna nodded in understanding. "You know Mom and I can run the restaurant, and Juana is a big help."

Consuelo's arms wrapped around Luna. "I know, and thanks. I knew I could count on you."

"When are you planning to leave?"

"As soon as I can get packed."

"That soon? Where will you go?"

"I'd rather not say right now. It's only for a few days, anyway. I'll call every day to see how things are going here."

"In that case, *que vayas con Dios*. But remember, if you need anything, I'm here."

Consuelo hugged her again. "I know."

After Luna had left the room, Consuelo began to gather clothes to take on her trip. She didn't want to be here when Ramón finished leveling his land. She just couldn't bear to think about it right now.

Ramón sat staring at the untouched cup of coffee sitting in front of him.

"I hate to say it, but you kind of had it coming, *hermano*," Raul said, taking a swig of his own coffee.

Ramón frowned. "I thought they'd be glad to see a mall around here, not to mention the extra income it would bring."

"We live in a small town, Ramón. That's why we

like it here—we enjoy the simple things. Tradition is difficult to give up. I'm surprised you didn't remember that."

Ramón leaned back and stared at Raul. "I've made a mess of things, haven't I?"

Raul shrugged.

"Even Rafael wouldn't speak to me yesterday."

"That's understandable. You're his brother, but he and Consuelo have been friends for a long time. We're caught in the middle."

Ramón nodded, acknowledging that fact. He sighed deeply as he stared out the window, recalling what she'd said to him just before she'd made her exit. *"I wish you'd never come back."* Those words had hit him like a ton of bricks. He'd thought that nothing could have hurt him anymore. But he'd been wrong. Her words had touched him at his deepest core, reminding him of why he'd left in the first place.

He thought of going to her and apologizing, but she'd probably have him thrown out of her restaurant. And what would he apologize for? For hurting her? For coming back? For robbing the townspeople of their shrine? He stared bleakly into space.

Finally, he rose, his coffee forgotten. "I have some thinking to do. I'll see you later."

"Good luck," Raul offered.

But luck was something Ramón wasn't banking on at the moment. What he needed right now was guidance.

* * *

It was late evening when Ramón arrived at his apartment. He went directly to his bedroom and paced. At one point, he stopped in front of the window that faced her balcony and bedroom. Of course, he hadn't expected to see her, but he wondered what she was doing right now.

A moment later, he stopped pacing. It wasn't getting him anywhere. It had gotten dark and he turned on the lamp in his living room, intending to turn on the television, but then on second thought, he went to his kitchen to get a beer out of the fridge.

He was in the act of getting a glass out of his cabinet when he looked out his window and froze. From his vantage point, he had a clear view of the tree, and right now, it looked as though someone had set some of the branches on fire.

Had someone gotten angry enough to burn it down? he wondered. But who would do such a thing? He slammed his beer down on the counter and ran down the stairs.

He was puffing when he halted in front of the tree. Surprise lit his features as he stared, surprised to see that the tree hadn't been touched, and he frowned. He could've sworn the tree had lit up.

He stood there for a moment, wondering if perhaps he was seeing things. He glanced toward his place. Suddenly, he didn't look forward to being alone in his apartment tonight, so he sat down on the lone bench by the tree. He smelled the earth and looked up at the sky. Stars were twinkling and he could make out the Milky Way. The sky looked so vast, he felt as though he was but a very small part of the galaxy at this moment.

He closed his eyes, enjoying the night. A cricket called his mate and a strong breeze sprang up.

"Mind if I join you, or would you rather be alone?"

He jumped and opened his eyes at hearing the unfamiliar voice. Before him stood an elderly stoop-shouldered man he'd never seen before.

"You looked awfully comfortable. I almost hated to bother you."

Ramón stood up. "That's all right. I have to leave anyway. Go ahead and have a seat."

"Well, now, if you leave, I'm going to think that it's on account of me, so you might as well just sit a spell."

Ramón waited until the man sat down before he sat down himself. He didn't know what to say to the old man, so he just sat silently.

"I have to hand it you." The old man smiled. "You sure know how to stir up excitement in this sleepy old town."

"I'd rather not be reminded of that if you don't mind."

"I'm not casting stones. Just wanted to say that I kind of feel halfway sorry for you. You've got everyone mad around here."

Ramón started to get up again, but the man's voice stopped him.

"Pretty night, isn't it? The stars are glittering, a nice breeze is blowing. I used to come here often, but it's been a while now. Getting too old to get around."

Ramón didn't want to talk about this old man's visit to the shrine—or anyone else's fixation on it. Maybe if he didn't fuel the man's conversation, he'd keep silent.

"I used to walk by here and I'd see Salvador sitting right where you are. He was younger than me, and he was a lonely soul at the time. I remember the day he told me that his dream had come true at last—that he'd met the woman of his dreams." He stopped for a moment and glanced toward the sky. "They married shortly after. He always swore that just as he was about to quit hoping, a miracle had happened and there she was. Strange how things like that happen." His eyes assessed Ramón again. "Anyway, they were happy for many years."

Ramón wondered if he looked as lonely to the old man as Salvador had appeared to him. "Are you saying he met the woman of his dreams because he prayed at this tree?"

The old-timer shook his head. "Nope. I'm saying that sometimes just when you feel your lowest, when you think that there's no use to hope anymore, that's when something happens. You just have to have more faith."

Ramón nodded, not certain what he was agreeing to and wondering why the old man was telling him all this.

The man sighed and stood up slowly. "Well, I'd better be going. These old bones are tired."

"Good night," Ramón replied.

Almost as an afterthought, the man murmured over his shoulder, "Oh, and don't worry, you'll know what to do when the time comes."

What an odd meeting, Ramón thought. Then, as if suddenly realizing that he didn't know the man's name, he started to call out to ask him, but thought better of it. What did names matter? It was a person's actions that spoke volumes, and the old man seemed friendly enough.

"A man's actions speak louder than words." Startled, he realized he'd just voiced his thoughts out loud. And his actions hadn't measured up nor been all that pleasant since he'd hit town.

In the quiet of the night, he surveyed his land. The moon was high, casting brooding shadows here and there. A strong breeze suddenly kicked up and touched his face and hair. He closed his eyes and listened to that same breeze whispering through the tree, causing its leaves to rustle, the sound strangely hypnotic.

He glanced up at the stars—tiny silvered lights looking like a jeweled box, shifting slowly in his vision. It would be a great night to be in a boat fishing.

He didn't know how long he sat there, but was shocked to realize that he'd fallen asleep. Now he felt oddly relaxed and rejuvenated, and chalked it up to the short nap he'd taken. He sat there a moment longer, wondering at the odd conversation he'd had with the old man and wishing he *had* gotten his name.

Well, it was too late now, he thought, as he got up from the bench and headed toward his apartment.

Walking up the stairs, he knew he was still too keyed up, too energized to go to bed. He started to pick up the TV remote but quickly changed his mind.

He headed for the kitchen, recalling he'd left a beer on the counter that he hadn't opened. He picked it up and set it back in the fridge. As he made his way through the *sala* on his way to the bedroom, he paused and glanced toward Consuelo's bedroom. Her room was dark, and he wondered if she'd gone to bed. For a moment, he wished he could see her and was tempted to go over there, but he nixed the idea. The memory of what had happened was still too raw.

Filled with nervous energy, he opened his closet door and reached down to grab a box he'd brought over from the ranch when he'd moved in here. He set it on top of his bed.

Recalling there was a strong breeze tonight, he leaned over and opened a window. Immediately, a breeze filtered through—the lonely rustle of the night wind.

He sat on the bed, opened the box, and began to rifle through its contents. He picked up a photograph album and opened it. There were photos of his family, of his mom and dad when they'd been younger, of him and his brothers as children and later as teens. There were also pictures of him and Consuelo during various stages of their relationship. He smiled as he stared at one in particular. They'd been to a Halloween party and they'd gone as Dracula and his Mistress of the Night. Suddenly he laughed as he saw the image of himself biting her neck as she glanced at the camera in horror—the look more comical than realistic.

He turned the page and his features softened as he studied her beautiful smile. She'd stared right at him as he'd taken the picture. The camera had caught the essence of Consuelo—beauty, intelligence, humor. He closed the album and set it aside.

For an instant, as he picked up a wooden box, he thought of the old man he'd met tonight and a sense of something indefinable washed over him. A sense of loss? Regret? He had run away seven years ago because he couldn't bear the thought of not being in Consuelo's life. And now, he felt a strong urge to live his life instead of running away from it. He wondered if the old man had been happy. Had he lived his life as he'd wanted to? Had he married the love of his life? Had he sired children? Ramón wished he could have asked him.

From some hidden corner of his heart, a thought pulsed strongly and he wondered: Could a person be lucky enough to find the same love twice?

He opened the box.

An eagle feather floated out and hovered in midair for a moment before it fluttered to the floor.

Eleven

He'd forgotten and left the window and the shades open all night, so the sun had awakened him this morning, bright and beautiful. He'd rushed through his morning ritual because he was anxious to see Consuelo before she opened the restaurant. After that, she might be too busy or too angry to speak to him.

Anxiety mixed with anticipation as he took off across the street. Now that he'd made up his mind to tell her how he felt—among other things—he couldn't wait to see her. Suddenly, he was somber, quiet, and miserable, and he almost stopped and turned back. What if she refused to speak to him? What if she hated him? He took another deep breath and quickened his pace.

Lena Morales was crossing the street from the opposite side and stopped him with a wave of her hand.

"Oh, I was just coming to see you," she muttered.

His eyes narrowed and he glanced toward the restaurant. "Can we make it some other time,

Lena? I'm in a hurry. Call me later," he said with a hint of impatience and then was gone, leaving her to stare after him.

When he knocked on the door, he was disappointed to see Luna standing there instead of Consuelo.

"She's not here," Luna said.

"When do you expect her back?" he asked, disappointed.

"I have no idea when she plans to return," Luna told him obstinately.

"Can you at least tell me where she is?"

"She wouldn't say. Thought you might try to force it out of us."

"I really need to talk to her, Luna." This wasn't turning out as he had expected, and his patience was wearing thin.

"I'm telling the truth. She didn't tell us where she was going, only that she would call us every day to see how things were going here."

"You mean she left town?" he asked incredulously.

"Yep, I think so, although she wouldn't tell me where."

He raked his long fingers through his hair. "Would you please do me a favor and give her a message?"

She stared at him, refusing to make any promises.

"Has she already called today?"

Luna nodded.

"Next time she calls, would you tell her I need to speak with her? It's important."

"I thought you two had said everything that needed saying," she replied angrily.

He sighed impatiently. "Just give her that message and tell her she needs to get back here before Saturday."

"Saturday?"

"I suppose if I asked you to keep something a secret, you wouldn't do it, right?"

"I have no secrets from my sister."

"That's what I thought. Just tell her I need to see her." Then, on impulse, "For what it's worth, I never stopped caring about her."

Luna looked at him suspiciously. "That may be, but you upset her."

"I'm sorry about that. That's why I need to speak with her."

"I'll tell her you came by."

He thanked her and went directly to Lidia's home. When he finished speaking to her, she reached over and patted his hand.

"Thank you, Ramón. I'm glad you came by. It takes a lot of guts to apologize."

"There's only one thing I ask," Ramón told her. "Please don't tell her until I've had a chance to speak to her."

"You have my word, I won't say a thing."

"Thanks."

Ramón spent the rest of the day at the ranch where he had lunch with Raul, and later, he took Diablo for a ride. They stopped at the river, and memories came flooding back of the times he and Consuelo had loved and laughed here. Her passion had excited him. He ached to hold her now. Would she ever speak to him again? he wondered.

It was early evening by the time he returned to his apartment. He thought about dining at Consuelo's Mexican Restaurant. Maybe Luna would have heard from her again. Would she give Connie his message? He hoped so, because he was going crazy not being able to speak to her. Despite his wish to have some news about her, he finally decided to stay home and fix himself a ham sandwich.

He was just sitting down to eat when the doorbell rang. He went downstairs to see who it was.

Luna stood on his doorstep. "I've decided to give you the benefit of the doubt. I have something to tell you."

"Come on up, I was just about to eat."

"No. What I have to say won't take long. It's a story you need to listen to. Afterward, I'm afraid you're on your own."

He motioned for her to take the chair in front of his desk, and he sat down as well.

Without further prodding, Luna told him everything: how at age eighteen, she'd come home and found Consuelo crying; how her sister had cried herself to sleep at nights and called out his name; how she had continued to love Ramón even when she was marrying Tomas. Luna left out nothing; she even spoke of their father's death.

"My father was old-fashioned and thought he was doing the right thing. He loved us, and his heart was in the right place. He couldn't leave this world without knowing that all of us would be well taken care of, so Consuelo had to take on that responsibility. I really believe that if you hadn't left town, she would have changed her mind. For what it's worth, there's never been anyone but you."

Silent joy coursed through Ramón's body and he smiled. "Thanks for telling me." He recalled that Connie had tried to explain at the river and he hadn't listened. He felt immense guilt and swore to himself that he'd make it up to her.

Luna stood up. "I felt you should know."

"Yes, thanks again."

As Luna made her way back to the restaurant, she didn't know whether she'd made things better or worse, but at least he now knew the whole story.

The morning sun, warm and brilliant, peered through a break in the clouds. It was a perfect day to go swimming, or attend a garden party. *Or be with loved ones.*

Consuelo stood in the backyard of her cousin Maria's home, holding a practice session with her whip; however, she felt none of the excitement or challenge she usually experienced when she practiced. Her movements were too slow, too lazy, and she couldn't concentrate. Her heart just wasn't in it today.

Had Lidia and the rest of the committee decided to have the festival after all? She hadn't asked Luna, and Luna hadn't volunteered any information. If the women had decided in favor of going ahead with the festival, then it would be held this coming Sunday—only three days away. Her heart gave a painful beat.

Not for the first time, she felt she should have stayed to see things through. She'd left everything in limbo and knew she shouldn't have run away; but the truth of the matter was, she couldn't stand to see the tree being destroyed.

She also felt remorse for what she'd said to Ramón about wishing he'd never come home. She hadn't meant to spout those hurtful words at him, but she'd been so angry, she couldn't have stopped them if she'd tried.

She coiled the whip and set it on a lawn chair next to her, then sat down on the ground, cross-legged, to think. She couldn't stay gone forever and she didn't want to. She already missed her restaurant and her family.

Twenty minutes later, she'd made up her mind to return home, and she hurried to pack what few things she'd brought with her. She hugged her cousin Maria one last time and thanked her for keeping her secret regarding her whereabouts; then, she called Luna to tell her she'd be home before dark.

"Welcome home, *hermana*," Luna muttered as they hugged each other. "I'm so glad you're back."

"Me too."

"Have you eaten?"

"Yes, a sandwich shortly before I left."

"Are you going to tell me where you went?"

Consuelo thought a moment. "Maybe later, okay?"

Luna nodded, respecting her sister's wishes.

"Everything all right around here? Any problems?" Consuelo asked, glancing around the large dining room. She was happy to be home.

"No problems." Luna hesitated for a second. "Ramón came to see you yesterday."

Consuelo stared at a couple eating by a window. "Did he say what he wanted?"

"I think he wanted to apologize."

"A little late for that, isn't it?"

"Maybe. He wants you to call him."

"Right now, I want to go upstairs and change."

Consuelo went straight upstairs and kicked her shoes off on the way to her bedroom, carefully avoiding the balcony. She didn't want to open the doors for fear of what she'd see when she looked across the street. The tree would of course be gone by now.

She walked into the bathroom and turned on the shower, then padded back to get clean jeans out of her drawer. She realized her hands were shaking and her heart was pounding. She sat on the edge of the bed for a moment and took a deep breath.

Bit by bit, her facade crumbled and she crossed her arms over her chest. Rocking back and forth, she reminded herself that she'd promised not to cry. However, she *could* grieve in silence. So she grieved for many things, for lost love and lost opportunities, but most of all, she grieved for the tree because it had stood as a reminder of a family who had died. Salvador had cherished that tree, had believed in the legend behind it, and so had a lot of other people. She grieved for them as well.

She drew a shaky breath and let it out slowly. She couldn't stand it. She had to see for herself.

She walked over to the French doors, opened them and stepped out on the balcony. Consuelo glanced toward Ramón's apartment. Darkness would fall in another hour, but she noticed that he had turned on a light in his living room.

Curiosity pulled her eyes toward Ramón's land. She couldn't prolong the inevitable any longer and she gazed toward the tree, expecting the worst. She would miss it.

Her heart began to pound and her hands were shaking. Happiness beyond words buoyed her spirits, and, unable to repress her excitement any longer, she ran down the stairs.

Luna was waiting for her at the bottom of the steps, smiling.

"Why didn't you tell me?" Consuelo asked a little breathlessly.

"Oh, how I wanted to, *hermana,* but I was sworn to secrecy."

Consuelo's enthusiasm was too bright to be ignored and she hugged Luna. "You're forgiven. Can you cover for me for a while? I have to go out."

"Of course. Take all the time you need," Luna replied happily.

As Consuelo hurried out the door, she called

over her shoulder, "Oh dear, I forgot to turn off the shower."

"I'll take care of it," Luna said.

He'd kept the tree! The words kept echoing in her mind. He hadn't destroyed it! She felt enormously relieved as she approached the tree. A young couple sat on the bench and Consuelo smiled at them, recalling how she and Ramón had been caught kissing under this very tree. And only recently, she remembered with a giggle.

Wanting to give the couple their privacy, she started to leave, but something caught her eye. Amid the old initials that had been carved into the tree, she noticed new ones. She peered closer and saw someone had carved the initials *RS,* and directly beneath them were her initials. She beamed with almost comical happiness.

Her heart soared. She had to find him, had to tell him what a wonderful human being he'd turned out to be.

She ran to his building and rang the doorbell, but no one answered. Trying the door, she found it was unlocked and walked in, calling his name. Still no answer. Disappointed, she ran up the stairs, hoping he'd be there. He wasn't and she felt strangely empty. She had to see him. She picked up the phone and dialed Raul's number, and afterward, Rafael's. Neither of them had seen him all day. She tried desperately to think of where he might be.

Her heart was pounding. *Please, God, don't let him leave again. Please.* She had to speak to him. Now!

She glanced around for some sign that his

clothes were still here, that he hadn't left her again.

When she saw he hadn't left town, she breathed in relief and closed the door to his closet.

It was then she saw it. On his dresser, tucked into the side of the mirror frame, was a feather. A twin to the one she owned. The one he'd given her.

She went over and picked it up. That feather told her all she needed to know. He still loved her! The day he'd brought the feathers to their spot at the river, he had glanced down at her and told her what a difference she'd made in his life. It was the first time he'd told her he loved her, and as they'd exchanged the feathers, they had pledged their love and souls to each other. Afterward, they'd consummated their vows by making love.

She walked over to his window and stared across to her bedroom, wondering if he'd been watching for her to come home.

Glancing down at the feather, she suddenly knew where he was. She ran down the stairs with his feather still clutched in her hand. When she reached her room, she grabbed her hat and keys and hurried out the door again.

By the time she reached the river, the sun was beginning to dip slowly down to the horizon. There were tears in her eyes, but they were happy ones, and she smiled.

He was there, gazing out toward the river. She hurried out of the car and knew that he'd heard her slam her car door, but he didn't turn around.

For a moment, she panicked. What if he never intended to forgive her? What if he asked her to leave him to his comfortable solitude?

She blinked and fought to dispel the cloud of doubt. Her courage was slowly unraveling with each step she took but she pushed it back, refusing to be deterred.

Recalling why she'd come here, she straightened her shoulders and continued forward. No more running away for either of them.

When she was within a few feet of him, she halted and stared in awe. The sunset was painting the horizon a red-orange tint, and she could understand why there were sun worshipers.

He wore jeans and a green chambray shirt, and his dark hair looked carelessly windblown. He was beautiful. For an instant, she glanced up toward the sky. *Father, if you can hear me, please help me. You have Tomas with you now. I need Ramón. I should have always been with him.*

The breeze ruffled his hair.

She took off her hat and pitched it toward him. It sailed through the air and landed close to one booted foot.

"It took you long enough," he said as he bent down to pick it up.

Her heart skipped a beat. "I had to take care of something. I had to make sure I didn't forget."

He turned and pinned her with his stormy gaze. "Forget what?"

"This," she said, uncurling her fist. Resting in her palm were the two matching feathers.

He closed the distance between them. When he

was within a heartbeat of her, he studied the feathers in her hand.

"Now how do we tell them apart?" His voice was husky as his lips hovered dangerously close to hers.

In her eyes was all the love she'd been holding back, love she would never hold back again.

She smiled. "Simple, mine has a red dot on it. Nail polish."

He returned her smile and picked up her feather. "It wouldn't make any difference, because I don't intend for them to be separated ever again."

His hand felt warm as he took her feather. He'd left his in her hand. Now as she clutched it, her eyes were bright with unshed tears. "Will you marry me?"

"I married you in my heart here seven years ago," he whispered.

She held up the feather and he touched it with his, and as they looked deeply into each other's eyes, her voice was filled with emotion. "As Father Sky and Mother Earth are my witnesses, I vow here before them and you, to pledge my love, my heart and soul to you—forever."

He repeated the same vow to her. Later, they would be married in a traditional wedding ceremony, but it would never take the place of this one. Nor would it ever be forgotten.

As their lips met, he whispered into her mouth, "I love you."

Consuelo's heart soared with happiness. The people of Sandera had their shrine and she and

Ramón had theirs. This river and this place in time would always hold a special place in her heart.

He laid her down gently on the soft meadow grass and they made sweet, slow love, consummating their vows. Two hearts, one soul, finally reunited.

Twelve

The festival usually took place on the church grounds, and this June, it was no different. Each year it was the happy duty of Father Miguel to supervise the preparations and give his blessing and thanks for another abundant year. This year, their shrine had been saved—they had much for which to be thankful.

Since Texas summers can be cruel, the men dressed in their casual or Western attire, while the women donned light clothing—cotton skirts and blouses or sundresses were the norm.

Noisy children swarmed like flies and darted in and out between their parents. Several charity booths with games, food, and drink stood side by side like identical twins, manned by volunteers. It was to one of these that Consuelo and Luna made their way. Consuelo had business to discuss with Lena Morales regarding a luncheon she'd booked at the restaurant.

"Come on, Luna, it's all in the spirit of fun. You helped these women in their cause, so it's only fair you should participate."

"But, Connie, I don't want a man," Luna grumbled. "And the only reason I've been asked to make the walk to the shrine is because there are only three other women participating. Esperanza said she wouldn't do it unless I made the walk with her. If you ask me, that smacks of blackmail. And just where are all the single women in Sandera?"

"I don't know, *hermana*, but pretend to be happy, because we're about to reach Esperanza. Doesn't she look sweet?"

Esperanza smiled and waved. "Hello, Connie . . . Luna. Isn't it just about the most exciting day today?"

"Yes, it's the best one I've attended so far." Consuelo smiled meaningfully, since she and Ramón were also celebrating their engagement.

Luna refused to comment and looked as though she'd rather be doing something else today.

"I'm about to go speak to your mother," Consuelo mentioned.

"Oh, I need to speak to her also." Esperanza turned to Luna. "Would you be so kind as to relieve me for a moment? I'll be right back, I promise." She stepped outside the booth so Luna could slip inside.

Luna stared at the ragged line of men waiting to approach the booth. "That's a pretty long line. What are you selling?" she asked, looking around.

Esperanza smiled. "Kisses. This is the kissing booth."

"Who's harebrained idea was that?"

"Mine. It's for charity," Esperanza said and winked.

Luna watched them walk away. Obviously there was more to Miss Fancy Pants than met the eye.

Over her shoulder, Consuelo silently mouthed the word "Behave."

"Hey, we don't have all day here."

That voice sounded familiar. She glanced up to see who it was. Of all the rotten luck. Raul.

Ignacio Flores shyly handed Luna his money and gave her a quick peck on the lips to the cheers of the men. Next came the cute guy she'd seen earlier when she'd bought a beer. She smiled and puckered up. Not bad.

Then it was Raul's turn. They stared at each other like two prizefighters circling the ring. "What are you doing here?" she asked.

He took a macho stance. "What does it look like I'm doing? I'm donating to charity, and from the looks of it, you could use it," he said, eyeing her denim short coveralls.

"It's for the church, but if you're going to be insulting, you can just keep your money."

He shook his head and said with a humorless smile, "I don't think Father Miguel is going to like you turning down my money, and he's watching us."

"Then let's get it over with," she snapped.

He leaned over, but she pulled back. "Your money first, cowboy."

"Avarice becomes you," he said, handing her his money.

Luna frowned. She would allow him a quick peck, then send him on his way.

As she leaned forward, his iron fingers closed over her chin and his lips touched hers. Surprised to find his lips soft and warm, she opened her eyes. His own had remained open, and as she stared into his amber gaze, she felt a flutter in the pit of her stomach. It felt as if some active ingredient had kicked into play.

He let her go, but there was a mocking glint in his eyes. "Not half bad, brat."

"I've had better."

"So have I."

An hour later, the event everyone had been waiting for arrived. Every person was excited and in high spirits. The procession of three unmarried ladies filed its way through the noisy crowd, causing the knot of people to press together in order to let them through. The young ladies were to walk from the church through the park and on to the shrine across the street. Once there, they would silently make their prayer known to the powers that be and then hang their garland tiaras on the tree.

All three women looked excited but nervous. They were missing one person—Luna, who stood on the sidelines looking bored and slightly tipsy.

"Luna, have you been drinking?" Consuelo asked.

"Just a few beers, Connie, nothing to get excited over. And it *is* for charity."

"Well, I'm proud of you for doing this for Esperanza. She looks nervous."

Luna snorted. "Actually, I think she's got everybody fooled; I suspect that sweet magnolia has a spine of steel."

Just then, Esperanza looked at Luna and motioned for her to hurry and join them.

"Well, it's nice that you've befriended her."

"I think it's the other way around. How long is this supposed to take?"

"Not long. Oh, they're starting the procession now. You'd better get on over there."

"Okay, I'm going, but all I can say is that someone owes me big for this."

Consuelo frowned as she watched Luna wobble slightly on her way to join Esperanza.

Although Consuelo wouldn't be one of the single women to make the trip to the shrine today, she was just as excited as if she were.

"Hello, beautiful," Ramón whispered from behind her.

Consuelo turned and touched his arm. "There you are. I was beginning to wonder where you were."

"We aren't even married yet and already she's possessive," Ramón said to no one in particular, although the man next to him chuckled.

Consuelo laughed and curled her arm around his. "You're darn right. I'm not going to let you out of my sight until after we're married."

There was a gleam in his eyes. "Wild horses couldn't drag me away. I'm never going to let you go, *cara,*" he said just before he leaned down to kiss her.

Consuelo thought she had to be the happiest

woman alive today. She had the love of her life by her side and she was never going to let him go.

Suddenly, a whistle rent the air and the crowd surged forward, eager to stay even with the young women as they began their trek to the shrine.

"Come on." Consuelo pulled Ramón along with the rest of the crowd.

The women crossed the street and cut through the park, then bounded across the street while relatives and friends shouted encouragement.

Anita Torres and Susana Hernandez were the first to reach the shrine. They were silent for a moment, then took their tiaras off and hung them on the tree.

Esperanza and Luna were laughing, teasing each other as they followed suit. Everything was fine as Anita and Susana walked off to join their parents. Esperanza had likewise stepped off the path to wait for Luna. All that remained was for Luna to do the same.

As the crowd continued to cheer, Consuelo waited for Luna to continue around the tree and off the path. However, Luna had just tossed her tiara on a branch, turned and was hurrying back, her attention momentarily caught by a little girl waving, off to the side. Luna smiled and waved back. Raul had just stepped onto the path when Ramón called out to him.

As Raul glanced back to answer his brother, he and Luna collided. She cried out as the force of the impact sent her reeling backward.

"I'm sorry, are you hurt?" Raul asked, obviously concerned. He held out his hand to help her up.

Luna frowned and slapped the ground with her hand. "No! And don't get any ideas; you're not what I ordered."

Raul peered down at her and shrugged. "Suit yourself," he replied and walked away.

"Luna! Are you all right?" Consuelo asked worriedly.

"I'm fine," Luna muttered as she stood up and dusted herself off.

"Maybe you'd better sit down for a moment."

"No. I'm okay, really. Ramón's over there waiting for you, so you'd better go."

Consuelo looked up in time to see Ramón speaking to Raul. "He wants to discuss something with Raul. Come on, let's go on over to the restaurant."

After the festival had wound down, everyone looked weary but remained in wonderful spirits. They had experienced their miracle. The tree would stand for many more years, God willing.

The town of Sandera was at peace once more and life was back to normal. Of course, it would be a matter of time before anyone would know if the four young ladies would find the love of their lives or vice versa.

Later, during a champagne and dessert reception at Consuelo's restaurant, where people stood chatting amiably, Luna told Esperanza that she didn't care one way or another. It took too much work and too much energy, and how did one know anyway when a soul mate appeared in your life?

"Mami says one just knows," Esperanza replied, as she searched the room for Raul. She found him and as they made eye contact, she smiled sweetly.

"Well, that doesn't tell me a whole lot," Luna said snidely.

Esperanza shook her head in agreement and sighed. "Now that Ramón is marrying your sister, that leaves only one Santos brother single. Mami says they have a stepbrother who no one talks about because he's in prison or the CIA or something."

Luna lifted a well-shaped eyebrow. "That explains a lot, Esperanza. Any guess as to which it is?"

"I'm not sure . . . CIA, I think. In any case, that leaves Raul single and he's kind of cute, don't you think?" Esperanza peered over Luna's shoulder just in time to witness Raul bearing down on them with two champagne glasses in his hand.

"He's kind of a klutz. All I can say is I'm keeping my distance," Luna said and took a step backward.

Esperanza cringed as the two collided.

Consuelo heard the sound of glass shattering as it hit the Spanish tile floor, and she looked to see where the mishap had occurred.

"Never mind," Ramón whispered in her ear. "While everyone's attention is occupied, I want you all to myself."

He grabbed her hand and led her outside. Just

as they reached the tree, she faced him and smiled.

"You wonderful man, why didn't you tell me what you'd planned to do with this land? I had to find out from the mayor."

"I've been trying to get you alone so I could tell you."

"So you've decided not to build your mall after all?"

"That's right."

"Are you sure?" Despite her smile, there was tension in her body.

"That I'm not going to build the mall? Absolutely."

"No. I mean are you sure you want to deed the land to the city?

"I've given it a lot of thought and yes, I'm sure. Now will you be quiet so I can kiss you again?"

"When did you decide?"

He sighed, knowing she wasn't going to give up until he'd given her an answer. "The other night, when I sat on that bench over there." He shrugged. "It just seemed like a good idea that the land belong to the town." He didn't mention the old man. He'd tell her about that later. For a moment, he remembered how the old man had told him he'd know what to do when the time came.

Consuelo leaned in and relaxed against him, her cheek resting on his chest. "Salvador would be proud of you. I know I am," she said in the darkness, her breath warm against his chest.

"What else are you?"

She lifted her head to gaze into his eyes and

her voice was a throaty whisper. "Very much in love with you."

He looked deeply into her eyes, his own misty with unshed tears. "In all the years we were apart, you were always there in my heart, in my dreams. There wasn't anywhere I didn't go that you weren't with me. So many times I wanted to come home, but I was afraid of losing you again. I'm still afraid, but I'm here and I want to grow old with you, *mi amor.*"

Tears were falling down her cheeks. "I never stopped loving you, and through the worse time of my life, you were there in my heart. I never lost hope. I prayed someday you'd return."

They held on to each other, knowing that it had indeed been a day of more than one miracle, and that out of the sadness and lost hope, she and Ramón had been reunited. At last they would be able to build a life together, and God willing, they would have children together.

They held each other beneath the protective shadow of the tree, and just as the setting sun kissed the earth, golden dust shimmered through its branches.

She rested her head on his chest, listening to his heartbeat, content just to be in his arms.

Somewhere above them, an owl hooted its approval.

Epilogue

The following spring, a large crowd gathered to watch; family, friends, even strangers craned their necks in order to get a glimpse of the happy couple.

Andy Perez smiled as he aimed his camera for another shot. After all, this had been the most talked-about wedding in years. It wasn't often a couple fought, then married on the same spot.

But then, it wasn't every day that the bride and groom were as beautiful a couple as Consuelo and Ramón. And as they stood beneath the tree, for Consuelo refused to be married anywhere else, the people of Sandera swore that as the marriage vows were being spoken, the tree took on a burning aura.

ABOUT THE AUTHOR

Reyna Rios is an award-winning author whose first book, a Romance Writers of America Golden Heart finalist, made the Waldenbooks best-seller list. Extremely diverse, she has worked for a politician and as a legal secretary for the city attorney's office, and she's been an extra in a movie, a main character in a mystery play, and was once vice president of a bullfight club. Reyna resides in Houston, Texas with her husband and daughter. She loves animals, music, reading, and watching romantic comedies of the forties and fifties. But what Reyna loves most is breathing life into characters and then sharing them with her readers. You can e-mail her at: ReynaRios@aol.com.

For a look at this month's
other Encanto romance

IN YOUR ARMS

by Consuelo Vazquez

just turn the page. . . .

The house was nothing like the old place down in Miami. Vacated by the previous owners, an older couple who moved to a senior community further down the New Jersey coast, it was about seventy or eighty years old. There was not a stick of furniture in it and the wallpaper was ancient. It was empty and more than a little lonely.

Its exterior was uninspired, to put it kindly. The brickface could've used a cosmetic makeover, and the same went for the kitchen and bathroom—although the latter had an old, quaint personality to it. Old and quaint was "in." The real estate agent, a man who looked like he'd dip into the cooking wine when the beer was all gone, touted the place's main assets.

The price was dirt cheap, the exact description of Alina Romero's house-buying budget. For the money, the prospective owner found herself with a master bedroom and two smaller ones, a fair-sized backyard choked with weeds, and a short walk to the boardwalk and beach. So, the house did have its merits and possibilities.

Sort of.

Tamara Romero, Alina's younger sister, inspected the master bedroom's closet and found more wire hangers than a family could use in a lifetime, along with some objects she didn't quite recognize.

"Eh, say, those come with the house," Arnold Peterson, the not-so-savvy agent, announced confidently.

"What comes with the house?" Mercedes, the baby of the family, peered into the closet over her sister's shoulder.

"The hangers. Those mothballs, too."

"Oh! So *that's* what those things are!" Tamara closed the closet door. "How lovely!"

Sensing a sale slipping through his fingers, Peterson blurted, "Really nice neighborhood, you know? Got a park and a ShopRite about a quarter of a mile from here."

"Hmmm. How far are we from a Home Depot?" Alina asked sweetly.

"Home Depot? Oh, not far at all! That's maybe another half mile down the highway."

"Good. That should be helpful."

"The school bus stops right down at the corner. School's a few blocks from here, close by. Great school system!"

"I hope so. I'll be working in it, come September."

The man's bloodshot eyes bulged. "That's right. You're a teacher. Where are you—"

"Harry Truman Elementary. I'll be taking over a fourth-grade class."

"Harry Truman Elem—well, *that's the same*

school!" Peterson flailed his arms in the air. "It's destiny! You and this house were meant to be together, Mrs. Oceguera!"

"Yeah, it sure is starting to look that way." She waved her hand in the direction of the hallway. "I'm just going to have another look at the dining room, if you don't mind."

"Not at all, señora. Look to your heart's content." Turning his attention to a small, brown leather notebook in his hands, Peterson scribbled something on a page with heavy, loud strokes of his pen.

Whatever is he writing in there, Alina wondered as she walked back down the stairwell. *Teacher plus proximity to school equals my commission on a house that's been on the market for two years.* Or he could've been paraphrasing P.T. Barnum: *There's a sucker born every minute, and at long last, I've reeled one of those babies in.*

"And it's desperation, Mr. Peterson," she whispered to herself, entering the dining room through the Mediterranean doorway, which she had to admit appealed to her. "Not destiny."

The house wasn't all that bad. She'd had a dining area in her house in Florida, sectioned off between the living room and kitchen. This was a dining *room,* not terribly impressive in size but with enough space for her cherrywood table and matching china cabinet, which were now in a rented storage space. And the room boasted two huge windows, through which the afternoon sun cast abundant golden light.

She sank down onto the dusty, mustard-colored

carpet and sat, hugging her arms around her knees. It wasn't the impetuous desire to look at the dining room again that had brought her down there, but rather the need for a few moments of solitude.

The last time she'd gone house-hunting, she'd been accompanied by her husband. She and Marco had toured three houses, at the most, before settling on the last one as their starter home. With two bedrooms and an aboveground swimming pool, it would suit them perfectly until they could build their dream home later on.

Those were the plans and dreams that would now never materialize. She'd accepted that . . . finally. Still, the whole situation was so strange, selling that precious home she'd shared with Marco and their son and beginning the process all over again, this time with her sisters.

Not that she didn't appreciate the gesture. Tamara had taken time off from work, and Mercedes had driven down from upstate New York to accompany her. Her sisters and parents were the reason she'd moved back to Jersey—that, and the importance of her son's relationship with his grandparents and aunts and uncles.

There was something about family that couldn't be duplicated. Being around her sisters again, she'd already overcome the feeling of being alone.

Footsteps resounded on the stairs. She remained seated comfortably on the floor.

Eagerly, Peterson charged full steam ahead, reiterating, "Reeeeeally convenient, being so close to that beach! In the summer, you pack a cooler and some towels, and you're good to go!"

"That's wonderful," Alina murmured, lost in her own thoughts.

"So, are you ready to go back to the office? I'll put that bid in for you in a jiffy. Tonight. I'll drive it down to the sellers tonight."

Mercedes glanced warily at Alina, and Tamara came to her aid.

"That's very kind of you, Mr. Peterson," she said softly. "I think my sister might want to take some time to think it over."

Instantly, the agent looked crestfallen. "What's—what's to think over? It's a steal at this price. Sure, I know it's not much now, but the place has great potential."

Alina cleared her throat. "Would you mind giving us a few minutes, Mr. Peterson?"

"No. No, uh . . ." Moping, he shrugged. "Go right ahead, ladies. I'll be, eh, outside on the porch. If you need me, holler."

As soon as he was gone, Mercedes sat on the floor beside Alina. With that same dulcet affection of the little girl who Alina remembered, she hugged Alina's neck and kissed her on the cheek.

"I love seeing you and Justin again, so much," she said.

"It's mutual, Mercy. And Justin loves his Uncle Quinn."

Tamara, ever the businesswoman, brought them back to the subject at hand as she slowly paced the floor.

"Don't let this guy pressure you, Alina," she advised. "And don't marry yourself to a house that quickly."

"Yes, I've been hearing you say those same words for about seven houses already." Alina subdued her exasperation. "Justin and I can't go on living in Mami and Papi's basement forever, Tammy."

"It's really not a bad house, you know?" Mercedes pitched in. "And that mortgage wouldn't drain the life out of you, either."

Alina was about to agree. Then Tamara asked, "And why do you think it's such a bargain? This is what you'd call a handyman's special."

Mercedes countered her. "So?"

"So? You know a handyman?"

"It so happens that I know *two.*"

"You do, huh?"

"Yeah. Quinn and Diego! I'll volunteer my husband; you volunteer yours."

"No, no, that's out." Alina shook her head vehemently. "I'm not imposing on anyone. I'll manage this myself. Somehow."

Tamara frowned. "You sound like you've already made the decision to buy this place."

"I think I should go for it, Tammy. I don't know." She tossed locks of her long, rich brown hair over her shoulder. "I don't want to keep living in my parents' house. I'm an adult."

"That's debatable," Mercedes teased.

There was a pause. Tamara glanced out the window, sighing. "It's just that I don't want to see you make any snap decisions. I mean, this house could turn out to be a money pit."

"That's why I need to hire an inspector to check out the property," Alina reminded her. "So he can warn me about the flood damage and the termites before I'm sitting in water and nibbled-up wood."

"True. But there's one thing an inspector can't tell you. And that is," Mercedes said, "do you *like* the house? Can you see yourself happy here?"

Alina rested her head against the wall. "Do I like it as much as the old place? No. That was home. But, can we be happy here?"

She stopped as soon as her throat started clenching. There were no memories in that old house, sweet and sad as they were. No reminders of her husband, whose life had ended without any warning whatsoever. She tugged at some frayed threads on the hem of her jeans.

Then she finished. "I think so. In time. Justin would love having his own room again. And I could put that third bedroom to good use, too. I should put the bid in tonight."

Tamara crouched down, joining them on the floor.

"Alina, it hasn't sold in two years. Be a little suspicious, at least." She smiled. "You, who are always so trusting! Sleep on it. Call Mr. Peterson. Tell him you'd like to see it one more time. And bring someone with you."

"I already did. That's why you two are here."

"No. Bring a *man*," Tamara specified. "Peterson's the type of guy that, even if a woman's an engineer, he assumes all she's thinking about is which color scheme would look best in the living room. You have a man there, barking questions at him left and right, and I guarantee the guy's coming up with something better than 'the mothballs come with the house.' "

Mercedes tittered. "I'll find out if Quinn can make it down here sometime this week."

"Why? We live a lot closer. Diego wouldn't mind accompanying you, Alina."

She warmed to the idea. "Okay. I'll wait then and come back—but at Diego's convenience."

"All right, then. Let's go break the news to Hanger Man!" Mercedes rose and helped Alina to her feet and then walked beside her to the front door. "You know what you need, girl? Some time to yourself."

"I'm a mother. Mothers don't get time to themselves."

"Now that's an encouraging thing to say to a woman who wants to join the ranks of motherhood." Mercedes laughed. "You've been through a lot this year, Alina. What's one little weekend?"

Temptation nagged at her. So far, the past year had been anything but a picnic. Between selling the house in Miami, moving back to the state she'd grown up in, and finding a suitable home at a reasonable price, Alina's nerves were on edge.

Between temporarily living in her parents' basement apartment, which made decent but cramped living quarters for her and her toddler son, and working in a new school in the fall, the stress was mounting.

"Quinn and I could watch Justin for you. It'd

give him a good idea of what to expect, if a pregnancy test says yes, after all."

"That could backfire, you know."

"No, come on. But back to you. Mami and Papi hardly ever use that house by the lake. Tamara and I are up there with the guys more than they are. I'll loan you my key, if you want."

"I have to think about it, Mercy. I have a lot to think about."

Having joined her sisters for breakfast that morning before meeting the real estate agent, Alina wanted to get back to Justin. At that very second, their father, Alejandro Romero, was engaged in his favorite pastime—spoiling his only grandson. Hopefully, both her sisters would announce their own blessed event that year. That would rightfully divide their parents' spoiling techniques among the kids, or they would go bankrupt in the process.

She left behind a disheartened Arnold Peterson, who seemed ready to drive his car off a pier at the postponement of the sale, and drove her secondhand Nissan to the highway. She drove slowly, taking time to notice the surroundings, which were only now becoming familiar to her again.

The South Jersey community truly wasn't a bad little town. Most of the homes were either brick or Victorian, and the majority of the shops were located on Main Street. The fragrance of sea salt scented the wind coursing through the car's open windows. A row of larger Victorians—bed and breakfasts—lined the streets facing the board-

walk. Farther down was the town's main claim to
fame: the Church of Christ, Resurrected, estab-
lished in 1872, the year the town was founded.

She'd returned to a year of four seasons. Alina
had missed that, living in Florida's never-ending
summer. The proximity to her job couldn't be
beat, either. As she passed the park, where four
teenage boys were enjoying an energetic game of
basketball, she thought about her son. Horizon
Beach appeared to be a good enough place as any
for Justin to someday call his hometown.

Maybe another tour of the prospective home-
stead with her brother-in-law, Diego Santamaria,
would help her make a solid decision. By now, she
was accustomed to being the sole decision-maker
in the family—a responsibility thrust upon her
three years earlier when Marco died.

But just because she was used to it didn't mean
that it ever got any easier.

The beauty across the room was Alina Romero.
Suave was certain of it.

Except that she wasn't a Romero anymore. Her
last name was something else now since she'd
married that good-looking, popular ballplayer in
school and moved down to Florida. But Tamara,
who'd recently renewed her longtime friendship
with him, would have adamantly disagreed.

Once a Romero, always a Romero.

"Daddy, watch out!"

"What?" He spun around in time to get bopped
in the chest by a Ping-Pong ball.

"Oops!" His daughter, Ellie, hunched her slender shoulders. "Sorry, but you weren't paying attention."

"Oh. No, no, I'm sorry, *nena*. You're right." Suave stooped to retrieve the ball from under the table and rolled it across to her side of the net. "I missed, so it's your serve."

"Okay, but you better not be letting me win. I want to beat you fair and square."

Ping-Pong had never been his forte. Evidently, it wasn't Ellie's, either—though the eleven-year-old hung in there, managing to keep the ball in motion. Suave bounced it over her slender shoulder.

"Are you playing Ping-Pong or tennis?" she scolded him.

"Your dad's getting old, baby. Tennis would kill me."

"You're not old, Daddy."

While she hurried after the ball, he looked around for Alina through the crowd of parents and kids.

It was definitely her. Some months had passed since he'd last seen her at Tamara and Diego's wedding. Alina had been assigned to one table at their reception, and he to another. They'd talked maybe for fifteen minutes. As the matron of honor, she wore a sky-blue dress with off-the-shoulder sleeves, which showed off her feminine shoulders. She had worn her dark brown hair up that evening, and he couldn't take his eyes from her smile or the simple gold necklace that drew attention to the kissable skin of her neck.

And why did he remember it that way?

Ellie caught him staring at Alina as she played a game of skeeball with her son. "You know her, Daddy?"

Smiling, he snapped out of it. "Oh, that's Tamara's big sister. You know Tamara and Diego."

"Yep. Aren't we going to say hi to them?"

"Sure. Sure we will. Why don't we finish our game first?"

"Because we're going to be late for the movie."

"We have time. Wanna play the video games instead?"

"Not really. Unless you want to."

Quietly, he set the paddle down onto the table. There was a time when a high-tech indoor playground like the Funhouse would've entertained Ellie for an entire afternoon. Now his daughter—the child Tracy had conceived with another man, yet given to him—was growing up fast.

She bounced the ball up and down with the paddle, bored. "She's Diego's sister, you said, or Tamara's?"

"Tamara's."

"Uh-huh. And she's like Tamara, too."

"Yeah? In what way?"

"She's pretty hot. *You* think so, anyway."

Suave made a big show of consulting his watch.

"Hey, look at the time. We're gonna miss that movie if we don't hurry." With a hand on her arm, he guided Ellie around the table. "And I don't think she's hot. Well, she is, but she's my friend's sister."

And that was who Alina Romero would always

be to him. The pretty, friendly, and elusive girl who crossed paths with him in the school corridors and at Tamara's home. Then, their conversations had been brief, about as long as their chat at the wedding.

"So, why are you looking at her like that?"

"Like what?"

"Like you used to look at Mommy."

This struck a nerve in him. "She's a friend, Ellie. No—a friend's sister. That's all. She's very pretty, but . . . the only one for me was your mom. And now, you're my girl."

Ellie dismissed his hand, which was tenderly ruffling her ponytail. There were traces of her father in her features, but mostly she was Tracy in miniature. The classic, turned-up nose dotted with freckles, the high cheekbones and soft blue eyes—all were from her mother. Even the habit of shaking her head to clear the bangs from her eyes had been mysteriously derived from Tracy.

"I'm going to say hi to her," she said. "It's rude to leave without saying hi, and Tamara will get mad if she hears about it."

"We'll say hi. I never said we'd . . ."

Alina and Justin moved from the skeeball game to a giant maze of tubes, slides, and mesh pits. Ellie was on her way over to them. Suave didn't know if his daughter was afraid to offend Alina, whom she'd taken a liking to, or if that little kid part of her couldn't resist the maze.

Kicking off his shoes, Justin got down on his hands and knees to enter the maze through the first tunnel, followed by Alina. Suave walked slower, taken by the sight of her tantalizing rear, clad in tight capri pants, disappearing through the tunnel's opening. Ellie followed moments later.

What he felt was attraction. He didn't have to be a rocket scientist to figure that one out. Alina Romero was seriously pushing all the right buttons in him.

And that would never do. Not Alina Romero, not for a thousand reasons. Firstly, it was downright weird. She was Tamara's sister, and he'd had a bone to pick with the eldest Ms. Romero for quite some time.

All three of them were in the gigantic maze, which took up an entire wall. He knew Ellie liked to hang out in these things, but they had a movie to catch. With resignation, Suave knelt and squeezed his six-foot-three frame into the tunnel.

Alina was his least favorite Romero girl. Tamara had always been number one. Mercedes had been the cute youngest kid he had loved to tease and hoist over his shoulder, threatening to throw her in the pool for being a little pest. She'd always raised a fuss, screaming for her dad, then punching Suave when he put her back onto her feet.

Alina was the one who deserved to get dunked and taken down several pegs. Out of respect to the parents, he had kept his mouth shut the time that Alina had put down Tracy to his face. Tamara had done the same—but her he forgave, again and again.

Which was none of Alina's damn business.

Tracy es una qualquiera. Forget her, Suave. Every

guy in this school, freshman or senior, has gone to bed with her, except for you. And you won't, because even she knows you're too good for her.

In fairness, Tamara had also said similar things about Tracy. *Everyone* talked about the heroine of his heart in those terms. Suave knew Tamara cared for him as a loyal friend, and she spoke out of concern for him.

Alina, on the other hand, was just the high and mighty princess, the pristine and popular good girl, looking down her nose at the bad girl he loved.

"Ellie! Ellie, where are you?"

Somewhere in the distance, through tunnels and slides, a voice cheerfully called back, "Right here, Daddy!"

"Right here. Yeah, right. Where's 'here'?"

He was too big for the maze. Claustrophobia set in, little by little. He was afraid of his shoulders jamming in the tunnel and of getting trapped. Crawling carefully, he emerged through the opening and fell straight into the mesh pit.

"Ellie! Ellie, I don't know where you are, but we have to get to the movie! I hate missing the beginning!"

The mesh was another disaster. There was enough room for most parents—those under six feet—to stand up. Suave couldn't even get a foothold. His sneaker caught on the mesh and tripped him.

"El-lie! Where are you?" Lowering his voice then, he muttered, "Oh, damn, I'm lost in this thing!"

A feminine laugh bubbled over behind him. Not in the mood for levity, he threw a glance over his shoulder.

"I'm not *really* lost. Just lost my bearings for a second."

The woman smiling back at him through the tunnel's opening, with her hair charmingly mussed, was Alina Romero.

"Suave? Is that you?" She beamed, delighted. "Fancy meeting you here. *Que divertido!*"

"Yeah. Very . . . *divertido!*" He tried to mirror the same enthusiasm through his embarrassment. "How've you been, Alina?"

"Fine, fine. And you?"

"Excellent. Never better."

"Good. Hold on. You look like you could use a little help getting out of that thing."

A small cluster of kids, ranging from six to Ellie's age, gathered outside and watched. Suave noticed that they were fully amused by the sight of two adults tangled up in the dreaded mesh pit.

"I'll bet you a dollar the guy doesn't get out," one of the boys told the kid next to him. "And they have to call the fire department to rescue him."

"Na, he's getting out. The lady's helping him."

"A dollar says he can't do it."

"Okay, you're on."

Alina struggled to hold back a laugh, releasing it once Suave reached the opening of the next tunnel and stopped to point at the betting kid's companion.

"Hey, he owes you a dollar," Suave called to them. "Make sure you get it!"

Slipping into the tunnel behind him, Alina bellowed out to be heard above the noise in the tunnel above them, "So tell me, Suave. You come here often?"

"Uh, no. Not too much. And you?"

"Often enough. I'm a little worried. I can't find Justin now."

"He's your son, right? Tamara and Diego tell me he's a sweet little guy."

She smiled. "Most of the time, that's true."

"Well, I can't find my daughter, either."

"Ellie's her name, no?"

"Yep. Ellie." *The daughter of the girl you called* una qualquiera *some years back.*

A term that came dangerously close to *basura blanca.* White trash.

"I hear she's a little doll, too."

"Thanks. Is that the end up there?"

"I can't see. Your—um—*your* end is in the way."

An extremely nice backside, at that, she thought. *Along with long, athletic legs.* Alina forced the thoughts from her head.

"Sorry about that. It's some kind of—circular thing, going around and around."

"Oh, that's it, that's it! That's the end."

"Thank God for that, because I have to find Ellie. We're going to a movie."

"And I have to find Justin. He's only four."

The last tunnel emptied into a portal, beyond which spun a drum painted black and white, its swirling colors creating a hypnotic effect. Getting through it would be tricky but not awfully difficult.

Suave stood on the portal beside Alina, crowding her in an area meant for smaller bodies.

"Think you can handle that?" she asked.

"That's kid stuff."

"I'm dizzy just looking at it."

He conceded. "My turn to help you."

Suave grasped her forearm, leading her into the final part of the maze. Then things went downhill after the first step, with both of them losing their footing. Alina fell first. Suave struggled against the laws of physics and lost, falling on top of her.

It was a tangle of arms and legs, and they ended up in a compromising position, with one on top of the other. Alina yelped and laughed, grabbing Suave's shoulders and saving his glasses before they slipped from his face. Her hand brushed against his cheek, and she felt the heat of his skin on her fingertips.

She saw black and white and the color red from somewhere—a fiery, vibrant red—and the brilliant blue of his eyes, much too close to hers. His mouth was moist, ripe for a kiss. *One kiss, from a man's mouth.* As he fought to help balance her, she leaned closer to him, reveling in the sinfully wonderful taste of his kiss.